COILS OF OVERKILL

The final book in the *Memory-Camera Project* trilogy.

By Steve Hammond Kaye

STEVE HAMMOND KAYE

Copyright Notice

Published in 2015 by:

STANDARDCUTMEDIA

publishing@standardcut.co.uk

COILS OF THE OVERKILL

TABLE OF CONTENTS

Thirty Four Minutes Dead
Book One

Gregory Vain, a pioneering neurosurgeon and part of **'The Memory-Camera Project'** is part of a pioneering team that develops the ability to unlock the frozen images stored within the cortex of the dead mind and to read the living, thinking brain. He must also fend-off erotic advances from the vampirical Marcia Levene to save his marriage.

Steve Hammond Kaye's neo-gothic techno-thriller of power, knowledge, violence, treachery and blood-lust enjoy the paginated battleground in this dystopian vision of the near future - *Thirty Four Minutes Dead...*

Thirty Four Minutes Dead
Book One

She'll laugh at your fire..., burn in your fire..., die in your fire...

The Scream of Feyer
Book Two.

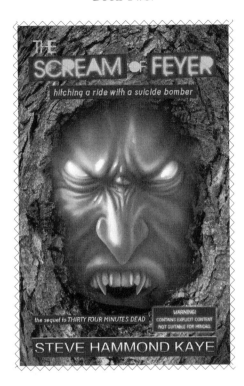

Twelve years have passed since the neurological atrocities were carried out by the Memory-Camera Project in 1998. The global population are now known simply as *the wasted* because they have had their brains altered in the womb or as an adult as part of *Prerogative Three* conditioning.

They now roam the cess-pool that once was modern society as mere living zombies. They are simply existing in a hell-on-earth world run by their decadent elite masters crazed and addicted on designer drugs, violence and sex.

The Scream of Feyer
Book Two.

The leader of the Memory Camera Project, Jess Wheeler wants to extend their research into other dimensions such as the occult. Can the human mind store visual information surrounding man's eternal questions? His private research throws up a true apocalyptic thunderstorm with the emergence of a devil from the dawn of time.

The Avoiders as they are known to the malevolent Memory-Camera Project members are mankind's only real hope.

"If Thirty Four Minutes Dead was a 'jolt' to the literary way of conceiving a story, The Scream of Feyer will prove to be a veritable 'thunderbolt'!"

BUY the Sequel to *Thirty Four Minutes Dead* and Prequel to *Coils of The Overkill* today from **Amazon**.

FUCK CREATION.
YOU STAGNANT WASTELAND.

 PROLOGUE

Salt Lake City October 25 2040 - 6am:

The bird circled high above the city, letting the desert gusts tear through its wings. It started to drop lower in an effort to avoid the savage winds of high altitude and when it was just a few metres above the ground, it veered toward the city. The smell of garbage acted as a homing device for a creature that had become reliant on human waste. When the disposal sites on the outskirts of the city were reached, the bird turned sharply in the other direction, flying away from the rubbish tips and back towards the sun. Another scent hung over the city that morning - the scent of death.

In the heart of the city a man walked the streets with purposeful strides that matched his determination. He placed a small Lilly - wreath on the shrine for 'The Lost Americans' and then proceeded onward to the churches that dominated the city. A droplet of sweat trickled into his left eye, appearing like a tear for a brief instant, before his gloved hand erased its presence. He continued to walk among the throng of churches, knowing that soon the right one would attract him. After an hour or so, an ostentatious building with a white - marble facade proved to be his *calling*. Quite alone he walked silently to the ornate doors and sank to one knee in front of another memorial. All these churches seemed to compete in mourning and lavish excesses seemed to be the hallmark of caring. He let a real tear drop from his sunken dark eyes. The doors then opened and a churchman of high office gently spoke to him.

"Each tear will bless their souls my son. We could build a river from the tears of thirty years and our crying eyes will help forge our path to heaven. Who did you lose on that blackened day?"

The man said nothing, staying on one knee with his head respectfully bowed. The churchman gently placed his right hand on the man's head and spoke again in an even softer voice.

"Let me see your face my son. Let me soothe your troubled mind. You have come to the house of the Lord and I will help you build a bridge to him. When our brothers and sisters were lost in Europe, the Lord provided. Lift your head my son and I will show you the light that reached out to them."

The man stood up to his full height, but when he looked at the churchman it was *malevolence* and not *piety* that shone from his eyes. He held the churchman tightly against the ornate entrance door and spoke a few words to him in a voice as deep as a canyon.

"Fuck your pity! I have brought you a fucking gift father."

With that utterance the man tore his gloved hand free and brutally punched the churchman so that the dignitary slithered to the floor. Then he reached inside his black jacket and retrieved a small glass phial from the pocket, before smashing it on the marble surface below him. The liquid ran across the marble with shards of glass arresting its progress. He pressed the churchman's face close to his and with both of them at ground level, he proceeded to lick the majority of the liquid up. The glass shards badly cut his tongue and as he smiled in the direction of the dignitary, blood seeped through his teeth. He made the churchman endure his bloodied, demented smile for a few more seconds before raising the terrified man back up to his standing height. He pinned his quarry against the door once again and gently cradled the churchman's head with his left hand. Just when his victim thought that his nightmare might be abating, a bloodied tongue entered his mouth with glass shards severely ripping his gums. *Evil* then spoke to him.

"Spread *our* word Father!"

ONE

Any place that goes by the name *Allgood* invites speculation and scrutiny. People wait for the tarnishing to begin, to return the place to less *exclusive* associations. Allgood Alabama was about to experience such a transition. It was about to regret having a name that was rooted in perfection.

Pastor Henry Sane had established the Allgood Presbyterian chapel as his regular preaching venue some eight years previous and now he was ready to alter his mode of delivery a notch or two. Allgood had been one safe haven where nothing out of the ordinary happened. The Pastor had waited his time and now his true colours were ready to take roost. Heaven help the God fearing folk of this backwater venue. Sane was going to unleash a new dark radical awareness in his teachings and his sermons would be the front-line oratory of his intent. As the Allgood believers took their pew positions, Sane began.

"The Lord has started to laugh at you my brethren, as you extol glutinous ways behind your false moral propriety. As obesity consumes you, vile stains are left on the pews of a tell-tale nature, of longing and lusting. In many ways it seems that you need to *free* your *bad* side. Even God is becoming bored with your apparent obsession with *do-gooder* ways. I say *apparent* because we all know what lies underneath - don't we?"

Sane paused for eighteen seconds whilst he scanned the congregation with his piercing eyes. He then continued with his polemic of insults.

"When God sees your clothing he despairs. One *dreamcoat* was allowed, but your gaudy lack of cohesion is an insult to him. Wise-up and heed my message. For eight years, I have swallowed and said nothing and now I must break this silence. You see, after eight years, a Pastor feels the flesh of his congregation and he knows the leaders and the losers. He can tell aspirations and motivations but he can go deeper than that, much deeper than that."

The next pause was very deliberate, because Sane's hammer-blow was approaching. In a mocking voice, he continued.

"I know that Lilly slept with John Richardson, who in turn had suppressed feelings for his sister and mother. I know that Glen likes guys and that Molly spins a trick with dogs! I know that Coryn can only cum if she plays the dominatrix and that Sheryl Hunter is actually a guy. I also know that Edith Erskine is addicted to cocaine and Bobby Larson to Icerlyxx. I know that most of you have bad dreams despite your rather ordinary exteriors."

Before continuing, Sane mopped his brow.

"This all makes me think, why the *facade* folks! All your happy colours and fixed smiles are just an illusion really. Why don't you let your bad side show more often with a truer representation of yourselves. Nice, nice boring is a dull drum beat of folks marching along to sterile conclusions and tethered fantasies. Time to grow a second skin my congregation, a second fucking skin!"

A hush fell among the assembly after the expletive was uttered by the Pastor. Then the sermon continued.

"Allgood has a current population of a shade under 700. Soon that will change my gentle people of Allgood. Thousands of young revellers are going to brighten the social horizons of this place. As a leading young Pastor of thirty years I say that this is good."

He then screamed *this is good* again and asked for an echo from his congregation.

"This is good, this is good" came the reply and the chant echoed around the ornate little chapel.

"God has told me that he will meet us in a new black and purple promised land - with Allgood as a new nirvana! I say this is good."

There was no need to prompt an echo response this time as the congregation were feeling a new found awareness and so responded as a matter of course.

Some of the crowd started to sway and Sane took this as a cue to build a frenzy among the worshipers.

"The young legions will bring an upbeat new tomorrow fuelled by the the dance of trance selection and they will deliver us away from the shackles of normality! They will rejuvenate our spirit and lift us to a higher realm of reality."

Sane looked as though he was going to continue speaking, but instead he released a high wining sound that grew in terms of intensity as it reverberated around the building. His eyes took on a manic quality with an electrifying gleam of intensity. He then arched his head upwards and reached out to some of his throng. The meat of his sermon then was laid bare for all to hear.

"My touch will purify, my eyes look further inside you. Let your evil seep out and I will usher your demons underground. I am your sanctuary and will lead all afflictions away."

Sane's eyes darted from person to person as he rhythmically moved his feet. His whole form started to writhe whilst standing and as his face glistened with beads of sweat his tongue briefly flickered across his lips. A sharp - eyed observer would have noted the forked nature of the said appendage.

"I seek one of you for curing my friends. This is *no* Jim Jones conjuring trick. Let me *heal* you."

A blind man stepped forward.

"How long have you been blind my son?"

"From birth sir. I am a Prerogative - Three victim."

"I'm going to spit in your eyes son. Do not worry. your god is at hand. Just take my hands as I anoint your eyes with my saliva. What is your name my son."

"Thomas Sir."

"Thomas, I will proceed. When I have given the spittle application, Laura will escort you to an alcove to contemplate the success of *my* work."

The congregation pushed forward as Sane applied his spittle. After the brief application Laura took Thomas away and the Pastor continued with his address.

"Decent people of Allgood, before we see Thomas again, I want to introduce you to a very special person in my life - my brother Troth."

All of the congregation looked to the back of the chapel where the angular features of Troth the first-born could be discerned. The dark-haired brother offered a cold half-smile as a return gesture for the congregation. He said nothing.

"My brother is a wanderer doing his work from state to state and we will see him here quite often in the future. He simply loves Alabama and what could be better than Allgood. Troth spreads our love across our beloved America and we have one final loving son in our triplet family. Scope is his name. He is a military man based in Vermont. Before we move on folks, give Troth one last hearty Alabama *greeting*."

The crowd extended another burst of applause…

After some more mundane sermon duties, Laura brought Thomas back to the pulpit area. Sane cut straight to the chase.

"Welcome back my friend. Tell us your story - do you *see* now?"

Thomas nervously pulled at the altar cloth and

with a trembling voice said.

"Is this what you call red?"

Most of the congregation went wild with backslapping or high-fives. Another chant was started.

"Pastor Sane - Miracle man."

After a short time Sane then asked for a brief period of calm, before continuing.

"Hey guys, Thomas has *two* eyes you know. Anything positive in the other eye my friend?"

"No just black as always Pastor Sane."

"Well I suppose a half-miracle will suffice for now my congregational friends! Christ did the whole ticket didn't he? Well I will live with being a half-Christ for the time being! Small milestones my brethren. I love you all."

With that line Sane let his throng depart. Most of the people were singing Sane's praises. The half-miracle left them on a high after the rather uncertain darkened entry. Sane was left alone to contemplate his success. His tongue flickered once more across his parched lips. He smiled when he contacted one of his handmaidens later that day. His tongue sent the woman into raptures as it simultaneously entered both the anus and vagina. This was one *party trick* he would never tire of!

He adored his Satanic status.

TWO

The fog swirled around DC like a choke- hold blanket that smothered the city. Kellerman was nervous. The President was going to hate the news that he was bringing with him. He drove to the appointed White House entrance and he turned into his designated parking space. Drizzle flickered across the windscreen. It was 21:09 and a cold sweat glistened on his brow. When he parked up his car, he was immediately escorted by two security officers. No names were exchanged. Everybody just knew their role and places. Kellerman merely followed in the footsteps of the silent pair. The trio then dipped down to a sunken area close to the parking lot. Here a fourth security officer took the lead and ushered the others to follow him.

When the trio entered the White House, Kellerman was blindfolded and lead upstairs towards the Oval Office. In the corridor next to the Oval Office, Kellerman was scanned via iris recognition. He was searched again and frisked top to bottom one final time. Eventually the blindfold was removed and the man was allowed to enter the hallowed walls of the Oval Office.

Martin Kellerman was a germ warfare expert who had met President Hudson twice before. He had on his person copious details surrounding the smallpox outbreak in Salt Lake City. He already knew that the *doomsday* clock that was hanging over the Utah venue was pointing towards the most sinister conclusion. He wondered if the President already knew of the ultimate *endgame* awaiting them.

Hudson greeted him and then began one of the

most significant conversations in American history.

"The smallpox crisis happened in Salt Lake City thirty-three days ago. It is defined currently as a localised epidemic. You are the expert Mr Kellerman. What in your opinion, is the current state of play pertaining to this outbreak?"

"A nightmare Mr President, far worse than I thought it would be. When we covertly released some of the same type of smallpox spores in Tokyo four years back, the virus was not fully bedded in or established. That was just our primary stage test phase. Only a few people died and it was quite easy to decontaminate the area. That was then, but our spore modifications have radically changed the situation this time around."

"In what way Mr Kellerman?"

"We have attached a barbed-taper to each spore, so that it locates, mutates and finally layers its presence in the air just above ground level. In short, even walking into these spores will contaminate a person. These spores will be able to hover in an air-based status for decades, unless they are radically dissolved."

"And how do you propose to do that?"

This question remained unanswered initially because Michael Kyra the Head of Security entered The Oval Office. He acknowledged the President and nodded to Kellerman but their greetings were mutually rather cold. Kellerman continued addressing the President's question.

"Well Mr President, in this context spore based alterations would involve creating mutant masking ingredients. These are extremely powerful spores and to alter their DNA structure a full modification of their stem-cell compositions would need to take place. Unfortunately we do not have time on our side. Your solution here may rest with Mr Kyra and ultimately Commander Scope because a military antidote may be needed. If this sounds too radical, we have got to remember that the Salt Lake City smallpox epidemic is increasing not decreasing!"

Hudson would have come in with another question, but Kyra interrupted his President for a second time. Hudson had a look of resignation come over him as Kyra addressed Kellerman.

"So you say that the smallpox epidemic is now unchecked do you Mr Kellerman?"

"I am afraid so Sir. We do not know how to put a block on the spore based degeneration. In short, the outbreak has become uncontrollable and out of control in Salt Lake City."

Hudson interjected with a key question to Kellerman.

"About 190,000 citizens currently reside in Salt Lake City. What is the likely level of contamination Mr Kellerman?"

"Current estimates envisage 46%, but that figure is rising all the time Mr President."

In a pleading shout Hudson cried "Why is it unchecked?"

The proverbial pin dropped as Kyra, Hudson and Kellerman observed each other.

Kyra broke the uneasy tension.

"I have not played my cards yet Mr President I await your decision with respect, but it seems as though science is not working in this instance. I mean biological tampering got us into this mess in the first place."

"You are being rather obtuse William Kyra. What exactly did you have in mind?"

"Well Mr President this is germ-warfare out of control really isn't it? I would not recommend throwing more germs into the equation and chemical eradication has proved rather messy in the past. I say that it is time to use history Mr President. Let's Nuke 'em."

Kellerman hated Kyra's uncaring words and he reacted accordingly.

"We are all Americans Mr Kyra. Epidemics are hardly joking matters - are they?"

"I wasn't fucking joking Mr Kellerman. You yourself said that the Salt Lake situation was deteriorating. Well as a nation we are not going to queue to be infected are we? Smart nations arrest epidemics by stopping the contagion. A Nuke may seem extreme to you, but one missile could effectively decontaminate us."

The President re-entered the discussion.

"Gentlemen, a home-Nuke does seem extreme, but let us examine today's Salt Lake footage on the video wall behind you."

The screen showed bodies piled three-deep in advanced stages of decay. Boils, welts and lesions ripped into the dead flesh and black rats gorged themselves on the more delicate body parts. Attempts to remedy the situation seemed to have been abandoned as a field hospital in one section of the city was looted and abandoned. All the medical staff in that hospital were dead and no hope for the future seemed to exist at all. This city had become a landscape of Armageddon with hell as the next stop.

As the images cross-cut to other parts of the city, some small groups in white decontamination overalls appeared to be trying to restore some form of order to the chaos.

They loaded bodies on to disposal trucks, but their work seemed laboured, as many of them showed signs of fatigue and damage to themselves. On occasions security personnel appeared to try and maintain a form of order, but their collective number was low and the gaps in their ranks invited street gangs to do as they pleased. In effect anarchy had taken hold in Salt Lake City and as the smallpox spores increased, the street cameras illuminated a decaying city for the dying and dead.

At that point the wind started to howl quite eerily and strong rain started to batter the Oval Office windows. The screened visuals had temporarily silenced the three office occupants and the seconds of silence held a *pregnancy* that was significant. Kyra took the verbal lead again.

"Mr President, Mr Kellerman, Salt Lake City has gone over the edge. The situation is irretrievable and the respective population are all doomed to die. We designed this germ warfare baby with others in mind but now we are gonna receive the full payload. A nuclear strike merely becomes a tactical cremation. An effective warhead will kill those spores through radiation poisoning and in that context the people are indeed expendable."

Hudson then added a verbal caveat to Kyra's words.

"This would be the end of Salt Lake City wouldn't it?"

"Yes, but it will eradicate a more widespread contamination." Retorted Kyra.

"No sponsor is going to put their brand name on America blowing up America! You forget Mr Kyra that all our missiles have brand tags that endorse their usage and appear on the missile itself. We have come a long way since Nagasaki's *Fat Man* and now corporate liveries are part of the nuclear missile design package. No advertiser wants to leave a legacy that is associated with blowing up part of our beloved country do they?"

The question was rhetorical, but Kyra answered it anyway.

"Four do."

Hudson looked alarmed and sought clarification. "What do you mean?"

"Mr President, not all the unbranded missiles have been destroyed. We have kept four in workable states without corporate branding, should such a situation arise like the one that we have in Salt Lake City. You did not know this, as we chose to select the override option sir. I am sorry, but this is how things are now."

There was a finality in Kyra's voice and the matter was not contested by the others. After a brief pause, Hudson moved the conversation along.

"You obviously believe in the Nuke option Mr Kyra. Would you follow a nuclear pathway in this instance Mr Kellerman?"

"No I would not. There is no guarantee that a nuclear missile would eradicate the smallpox spores - it may spread them further with a cloak of radiation adding to the contamination."

Kyra started to get impatient with Kellerman's position.

"Do you remember the Ebola outbreak in 2028 Mr Kellerman? America did nothing to arrest the contagion or at least nothing radical and 18,000 Americans died as a result. In our current crisis, a nuclear blast could well purify Salt Lake City."

Kellerman spat back a reply.

"If purification is 200,000 murders, give me a *fucking* gun Mr Kyra! I do not want a part of this madness! Where is your logic here? You castigate the 18,000 Ebola deaths and yet you recommend an A-bomb mortality figure that may be ten times that amount! Were is your consistency Mr Kyra.?"

As the two men's tirade became more hostile by the minute, Hudson chose to administer his token casting verdict.

"Gentlemen, I beg you to calm down a bit. Either conclusion will be tragic as thousands of our fellow

Americans will be dead or dying. The visual footage that we witnessed did indeed highlight a nihilistic world without any hope. The people appear almost beyond any help and so I return my attention to the location itself - the real cradle of the contamination. With this in mind, it is my conviction that this location must be dealt with to a degree of primary importance. All the buildings of Salt Lake City must be obliterated and yes Mr Kyra a massive nuclear strike could be our best hope in that context."

Hudson paused as the gale outside subsided slightly. This created a bizarre form of synchronicity and as the president waited to compose an end-line, Kellerman beat him to the draw.

"What about the survivors of the epidemic Mr President? They survive pestilence and then we Nuke them. This is hardly part of the American way of doing things is it?"

"No Kellerman, but I do now veer towards Mr Kyra's point of view. Nuking the city will be the lesser of two evils. We have days now not months gentlemen. I will give the order to make a missile ready. May God forgive me for this decision, but we have no other choice in this instance. It must be nuclear cleansing this time. We built the germ spores too well for any other form of decontamination to be viable. Mr Scope's reactionary force will be informed accordingly."

Kyra claimed the last words as dawn approached.

"You have seen the light Mr President. Nuclear cleansing is the only way. God Bless you Mr President. God Bless you America."

THREE

Five days after the Oval Office meeting, Kellerman was still rather disillusioned. He felt that his expertise pertaining to the Salt Lake City crisis had been disregarded. In his eyes, he felt that Michael Kyra had bullied the President into a Nuclear Submission and to say that he was fucked off about the situation, would be one great understatement. He had woken early that morning and had decided to walk around the scenic boating lake that was close to his house. This place inspired him and the peaceful solitude of the location was cathartic in reducing his pessimism. He skimmed a small stone across the lake, imagining the ripples on the water to be the indents that he would like to put on Michael Kyra's face. He could at least dream equalisation and alter reality from his envisaged fictional netherworld. As the pebble sank to the bottom of the lake, he scowled at reality.

He continued walking around the parameters of the lake, with his hardened outlook being softened slightly by the aesthetic surroundings. Kellerman thought about his 15:00 meeting later that day with The Memory Camera Project. He enjoyed working with this organisation, performing an advisory role with regard to *causes of death* factors and *decomposition rates*. Whilst Kyra and his security cohort always seemed to undervalue Kellerman, (as the Oval Office meeting reiterated), The MC-Project conversely welcomed him with open arms. This American organisation was initially owned by the UK and it had a rather chequered history, mixing great pioneering neurological work with more questionable cortex claims that were open to dispute. When the UK was wiped out after the mass contamination of Europe, America ran the MC-Project on its own.

An expert 6-person team ran the project. Sharmilla Hendricks and Thane Costa-Mendez were the joint leaders of the project. Vincent Perry and Jasmine Silver were experts in neurology. Paul Santorini was a laser extraction genius and John Galten an expert in digital conversion, completed the team. These six scientists were assisted by other researchers on occasions and Martin Kellerman had one such supporting role.

Kellerman was picked up at 14:30 and driven the short journey to the MC-Project headquarters. He received a very warm welcome from the beautiful joint-head of the project. Sharmilla was half Indian-half American and the appearance of this twenty-eight year old was more catwalk than science lab. Her beauty was beguiling though and as soon as she spoke an intellectual confidence exuded from her. Sharmilla had a very choice linguistic repertoire and her welcome to Kellerman was as succinct as ever.

"A pleasure to see you as usual Martin. Our project always seems to benefit from the forensic underpinning that you bring with you. We are most grateful my friend. Can I bring you any refreshments?"

Kellerman smiled, but declined. He was keen to ascertain whether there was any pressing business that he could help the project with.

Sharmilla then told him that a current lull had happened as far as direct physical brain explorations were concerned. She then softened this blow by stating that his forensic expertise would be needed again very soon.

The two of them conversed for a bit longer and Thane Costa-Mendez joined them for a short time. All three of them remembered when the MC-Project had been celebrated as the biggest ever neurological discovery. Suspicion had then clouded that status somewhat and more lean pickings had been the result. Whilst America still viewed the MC-Project as important, it did not elevate the organisation as pivotal anymore. The black clouds of a dead Europe had seen to that. After a final exchange of pleasantries, Kellerman decided to forgo the offer of a lift home and chose instead to walk the short distance to his locale. It was now 19:07 and twilight had started to claim the sky.

When Kellerman reached the crossroads - the halfway point of his journey, he opted to take the pastoral route that was more scenic than the other options. They knew he would.

He reached a fern-fringed glade and Kyra's men closed in. To Kellerman's left six uniformed security staff barred him access and behind him a further six tracked his every step. Dense thorn trees flanked the group of people on both the left and right sides. Kellerman was trapped. Silence sucked in the occasion - an evil portent if ever there was one. Everyone stood transfixed for about fifty seconds Fear then started to ebb into the psyche of Martin Kellerman and he spoke first.

"Oh come on William. It was just a disagreement man!' Just different opinions you know."

Kyra centred his position with a face as unyielding as any cold eyed killer. As steel coursed through his veins, he spoke.

"Yes Martin a disagreement, in front of our fucking president!"

"Oh come on man, he's just a fucking puppet - you know that!"

"You told him that - did you?"

"Nobody does. You know that. Why the heavy security presence.?"

"They all want to see the demonstration. Twelve private invites and all that fucking jazz. You know how it is."

"What demonstration?"

"You'll find out Mr Kellerman. After all, you are *our* star, our first trialist so to speak. Now it's time to wear this."

Kyra's men pinned Kellerman to an large tree and the security chief then placed a black fencing - mask over Kellerman's head. After Kellerman was fastened in the required bound position, Kyra retrieved a fist-sized black metal object from his security coat. The object had grooves cut into the sides and it had a lustre that gave it a rather curious glow. At this stage the object seemed relatively harmless and it was tied to Kellerman's left flank. Kyra quietly approached Martin Kellerman. His words were typical Kyra and not a trace of sentiment existed in his heart.

"Time to turn you inside-out Martin! Meet the Excoriator my friend. This will be a visual that we won't be sending home to mother!"

With that line, Kyra smiled at Martin Kellerman and after checking the tightness of the black fencing mask, he turned to his favourite cohort member and yelled ACTIVATE.

Nothing happened initially...

The security cohort held their breath in unison and Kellerman twisted uneasily- still bound to the tree. He quickly realised his brief advantage and delivered a memorable riposte line, dulled slightly from being within the mask.

"Hollow fucking party Kyra!"

With that line, Kyra kicked him in the testicles and the Excoriator was set in motion.

Slowly the Excoriator started to tunnel into the

skin of Martin Kellerman and the machine started to spit strands of flesh onto the undergrowth carpet beneath them. The dried dead leaves became red in an instant. Kellerman started to scream in terror and the said screams reached a new amplified pitch as the machine ploughed through his body. Occasionally the Excoriator jarred as bone obstructed its progress, but then lumps of bone started to be spat out too as the machine gathered pace. At this point Kellerman lost bowel control and temporarily lost consciousness as some of his internal organs were spewed across the glade floor. The Excoriator then started to zig-zag through the torso and the brave man breathed his last whilst still pinned to the tree. When the noise of the machine abated, it was replaced with the sound of manic laughter from the security cohort. They were placing bets on which part of Kellerman would fall off first. Nobody won this bet though as the Excoriator came to an abrupt halt when it got wedged inside Martin's rib-cage. Efforts were made to restart the machine on other parts of the victim's body, but the prototype needed to go back to the drawing board - for a while at least.

Kyra wiped the blood from his combat boots. He was *living the dream* of being the head of security. As Kellerman's body was thrown into the bushes, Kyra led his men away from the clearing. It had been a great sport and he could now concentrate fully on nuking Salt Lake City.

Sharmilla had slept uneasily. The Autumnal sunshine was a weak insipid yellow. The woman started to gather her thoughts, although not yet her clothing. As she walked naked to her rooftop window as her partner's laboured breathing provided a rather bizarre dawn soundtrack. He slept on as she wrestled awkwardly with her silken dressing gown. She scanned her mobile and saw that she had several videograms, perception-tunnels and emails. As she surveyed the list of contacts, one message stood out.

It was a laser-tracker gram from a Head Doctor that she had never met. She was curious and activated consumption mode to review this visual message.

The images had a scratchy, monochrome finish and the frail old man who was the sender, had an appearance that seemed to echo this poor production.

Staring straight at the viewer he began his message:

"When you receive this, I will be *dead*. You see, my cancer is an impatient-guest and waits for no man. Thirty years ago, I was the Chief Doctor at a birth, as I was for hundreds of births during my career. This was no ordinary pregnancy and the birth itself continued this rather darkened conception. The Mother's name was Marcia Levene and the Father's name was never stated as far as I know. Triplets were delivered in this instance, but I repeat that this was no ordinary birth. My Memory-Camera and Mindsight will both have captured the evidence. It is unprofessional for me to cast a verdict about what took place on that night thirty years ago, but nothing in my entire medical career has come close in matching the unusual events surrounding this triplet-delivery. I have made specific instructions that I will not be cremated after my death. Just make sure that you Memory-Camera scientists do the honourable thing here. God may help science on this occasion, but I fear that he might be rather outnumbered. Do your work."

The message ended and Sharmilla's researching work began. She contacted Thane Costa-Mendez.

"Thane, I've just received a D.A.D (Delivery After Death) message from an old guy - a senior doctor taken out by cancer. It sounds as though he has left us something that we should see - at the front-end of his dead mind. Can you call Jasmine, Paul and John so that we can perform a full exploration. We will try the main neurological vault first as periphery mindsight may add some confusion on this occasion. Address details have been appended as an attachment, so I am going to get Vincent Perry to organise the corpse collection this time."

Thane had one key question for Sharmilla.

"Thirty years is a long cold - case Have you got any more details to go on?"

"No I'm not even sure if crime is an issue here. The guy quotes God and calls on us to do the *right* thing - whatever that may be. I hope that he has captured enough HV's (Heightened Visuals) to help us on this one. I guess that those answers will unravel when we get inside his brain. Let's go find our corpse Thane.."

Vincent Perry located the deceased at Stanford morgue Lower East Side. He had taken a print from the D.A.D for identification purposes. As he opened the storage ice chamber, he saw the frail old man - the correct match. He verified the likeness, signed the respective corpse clearance forms and then wheeled the dead doctor to a waiting MC-Project vehicle. The venue for this full brain exploration was an unobtrusive building within the Georgetown sector of DC.

An hour later Sharmilla and Thane led the others into the exploration room. The back wall was primed for digital conversion purposes and the corpse on the exploration table was wired electronically to back wall receiver points. Laser extraction masks were in evidence, as were tools to enable Neuro-surgery. Two display screens flanked the table on each side. The lighting then switched to the favoured cobalt blue that the project staff preferred.

Jasmine Silver started to wrap the skull of the dead doctor with gossamer thin strips of electronic padding. She coated each strip with a responsive fixing adhesive that bound each strip to the skin of the dead man's cranium. In a short time there were more adhesive strips than naked dead flesh. On a given signal John Galten was given the green light to digitally convert Jasmine's work and an ethereal glow emanated from the skull of the dead doctor. Sharmilla requested each exploration participant to put on a laser-extraction mask at that point.

As weak electrical charges were pumped into the dead subject, Jasmine started to knead the dead brain. This should make a urological response easier to initiate. Once Jasmine gave Sharmilla the completion affirmative, all eyes turned towards the biggest display screen to await the arrival of the heightened visuals.

After a brief pause, the screen crackled into life. Now we would find out what images the dead doctor's mind had stored.

The initial visual captured a hospital delivery room. It was empty at this stage, although the viewer could hear the footsteps of the doctor as he prepared the delivery apparatus.

A heavily pregnant woman was then guided into the room. She looked fraught with worry. A medical orderly gave her some name tags and then he fixed a bigger *Marcia Levene* sign above the delivery bed.

There were no anxious relatives, no doting husband and no other expectant mothers nearby. A rather surreal quiet isolation hung over the scene. There was no panic and everything seemed to have a preordained quality attached to it. Levene changed *that* in an instant, with one guttural shout.

"MY WATERS HAVE BROKEN"

The proverbial mad rush then ensued and Levene was rushed to the delivery bed. The eyes of the dead doctor had captured the scene very well. A temporary calmness had returned to Marcia and this was a rather radiant quality in the context. Her next shout shattered this illusion.

"Fuck, fuck the pain-this is fucking *killing me*! Fucking do something doctors! Fucking help me!"

As some doctors held her down she thrashed her head from side to side. Her eyes were now bloodshot and her breath was being released in rasping grunts. She raised her frame higher on the bed as she had her first wave of severe contractions. She screamed as she entered this new pain threshold and she bit into the wearers of the red velvet robes who now seemed to be appearing on all sides achieving a dominance over the traditional white uniformed doctors. Levene was in far too much pain to ask who the new red-clad helpers actually were. As Levene's contractions intensified further she sunk her nails into the back of one of the red velvet helpers. Although Levene drew blood, he just smiled, eager for the impending arrivals of the satanic triplets. She became angered by his smile and spat blood at the man in red. Then her contractions reached a new zenith and Troth fought a frenzy in her womb to secure the passage of the *First Born*. His mother's blood ignited the fire in his dark satanic veins. No brother was going to take his place - he was the chosen one and he moved nearer to the vaginal gate.

"HEAD ENGAGED" yelled the chief doctor.

Levene looked upwards as agony conditioned her every movement. The head of the first born was prized out of her vagina and grey eyes scanned his immediate surroundings. Baby blue eyes were not invited on this occasion.

The child had a double tongue - one of normal size and a smaller forked one underneath. He had been born with nails and a penetrative stare that challenged the onlooker. No crying took place just the odd hiss as his coil was cut. The mother moved her hands to soothe the first born but the child resisted pulling away and surveying her from a rather eerie posture on his front. He examined his fingernails again and stared through his mother as if she wasn't there. Levene sobbed into her pillow and moved away from the creature that she had released. Then she recoiled in another bout of agony as the second son started to follow his brother's route out. This child wriggled for some hours near the womb entrance stalling delivery as he scented her blood. When the second son's head emerged another forked tongue briefly lapped at the mother's skin and then he was pulled out with angry tears announcing his presence. On seeing the second child Levene once again looked to the heavens. The second child like his brother was human for the most part but forked tongues, nails and grey eyes signified danger to Levene and she knew that their father *Klue* had a greater shaping in their destiny than she did.

After her terrible pain and the appearance of her first two sons, Marcia started to slip away The third child was still inside her, but she could push no more.

As her eyes approached final closure she whispered her last words.

"It's time Greg."

So ended the life of Marcia Levene - to live and die in the MC-Project *forever*.

The doctors then rushed to free the weaker third child from the dead mother. As the doctors tugged at the half released child, the first born clambered over in an effort to release the last son. He was clumsy through his inexperience, but he managed to lay a hand on his brother nonetheless.

This child cried as he emerged and one could tell from the outset that he was more of the mother.

Sharmilla turned to her project colleagues.

"That was thirty years ago guys. We will track those sons over the last three decades. One thing is for certain though - there are three *Lucifers* on the run with a thirty year headstart!"

FIVE

December 2 2040 and a double-rainbow stretched across the Vermont skyline. This often signified good fortune, but on this particular date a black chapter for American history would be forthcoming. William Kyra's missile was now in readiness and his security cohort ringed the launch site in in their hundreds. One thirty year old man did get clearance to pass through the black-clad ranks though. He was Morgan Kyra the son of the Head of security. His angular features and cold blue eyes had the same piercing intensity as his father's eyes did and his purse lips remained sullen usually disallowing a smile or softer expression. On his back he carried a large haversack. For Morgan this day would represent a treasured equaliser, if he got his way and his father's approval. He walked through some fresh puddles in his upmarket brogues, catching his reflection briefly in the rippled water. He got near to his father's security headquarters. Two seven-footers let him pass with simultaneous nods of approval. William Kyra then strode out to meet him flashing a brief smile like a rare commodity. Morgan was ushered inside and William Kyra spoke first.

"Good to see you Morgan. We've got a rather muted launch day because of our target, but always remember my son that on this day we *cleansed* Salt Lake City - not destroyed it."

"I got you dad. When can I see that crazy white missile that you have been raving about?"

"Right now son - just follow me."

With that line William Kyra led Morgan down through a cellar passage to the lift that was waiting for them. They dropped down four floors and were greeted by some more of the security cohort as they got out of the lift. Both men were flanked either side as they walked and then they dropped down four flights of stone steps with labyrinthine contours. Morgan said later that day that these steps had the claustrophobic feelings of a Piranesi catacomb. They continued onward after their temporary dark illusion. They were accompanied into another lift and here they descended down another five levels to eventually reach the base level. They were quite thankful to get out of the lift. The base level was a hollowed out cavern. This cavern was very high and extremely wide. Standing tall as a beautiful unbranded white centre-piece, stood the missile. Appearing rather svelte in it's uniqueness, the missile reached a height of just under twenty metres. The dark grey of the cavern rock and the virginal white of the missile made for an amazing contrast. Morgan couldn't contain his enthusiasm.

"Yo dad this is a dream! No squat ugly bombs like Fat Man or Little Boy! This is like a majestic rocket. Check out how it gleams and it's beautiful height. This is a missile-masterpiece! How is this baby going to get out of this cavern?"

Pleased by his son's enthusiasm, William Kyra went into descriptive raptures.

"She is canted to a 45 degree angle and then lifted toward the cavern ceiling via the hydraulic Stanga lifting cranes. The ceiling then partially opens and then this baby is activated and finally launched. Usually in this Vermont setting we test-fire outwards over the sea, but that has had to change in this real instance. The flight of the missile will be overland on this occasion until detonation, half a mile above Salt Lake City. This missile is a B90 three Megaton plutonium-based device and her journey time is estimated to take a shade over 2 hours. That's 2,333 lightning - quick miles and boy what a payload at the end. What's in the bag Morgan?"

"Black adhesive transfers Dad."

"To what end?"

"Well you told me that you were in charge of this amazing white missile unmarked and unbranded. That got me thinking. Do you remember when I was a sophomore student at MIT there was a guy called Meade from Salt Lake City who kept plagiarizing my fucking work. He failed one too many units in the end and dropped out, but both of us were downgraded in year two because our tutors said that they did not know who copied who. The transfers are my revenge Dad - to appear on the fucking missile if that is alright with you?"

"Let me see them then."

Morgan opened his bag and placed the black single sided adhesive transfers on the white table that they sat next to. In ornate ten inch letters the transfers spelled out...

...CATCH THIS MEADE.

Morgan then spoke again.

"I recovered my grading profile after that sophomore blip, but that would never have happened if it hadn't been for that cunt Meade. A missile shouldn't fly totally unmarked Dad. Let it carry my revenge please."

"Granted Morgan. Put your transfers halfway up the missile. The Launch is timed for 16:01. We are going to watch it together - father and son."

Morgan climbed up one of the Stanga cranes and placed the respective letters in a small line around part of the missile. The effect was neat and ordered.

At 15:59 everyone was in place to watch the two minute countdown. If the altered tracking-points had been put in correctly, the missile would initially fly seawards, but would then come back on itself to begin it's Salt Lake journey. The countdown ended and the roof parted to allow the white nose-cone of the missile to slowly push through. Then speed took over and the missile flew straight out of the cavern in a beautiful arc whilst settling on the course co-ordinates. It then turned as forecast and Morgan applauded as it flew directly over their heads. Death looked quite beautiful in this instance, very beguiling though as this was the most dangerous Nuke ever sent thus far.

On she flew a couple of miles above ground level. She could be seen by millions of Americans as she undertook this dark journey. She slowed down just over Wyoming to allow time to build both speed and height as she started to near the Utah detonation venue.

On the ground in Salt Lake City most people were largely oblivious to any further bad news. Society had largely seemed to have cut them off and the small improvement in the smallpox statistics had been hidden by the dominance of previous ill tidings. The citizens of Salt Lake City briefly looked skywards and then they looked no more.

SIX

William Kyra had carried out the nuking of Salt Lake City with a smile on his face. Only one person could have intervened and stopped Kyra's plans. Commander Scope was the said person. After a succession of quick-fire promotions, he now held the title 'The Head of the Military'. Despite his senior rank he had chosen to leave Kyra's decision unaltered. In effect Scope had been Lake City's last hope. Scope's brother Troth had contaminated Salt Lake City in the first place and a nuclear detonation became a radical way of getting rid of the evidence. Scope was the most stable of the satanic triplets. He had more of his mother's genes than the other two brothers.

Troth was the twisted First Born son who led the others from afar. In many ways it was the second son that seemed to exhibit the most traits of madness. Sane was anything but his namesake and his depravity knew no boundaries. He had been right about the influx of the purple and black clad revelers (sic) and they swamped the region close to Allgood in their thousands.

Four distinct groups made up the Allgood Gathering' but three of these groups thrived on the dark motivating factors behind their formation.

'Judas Silver Trail' were the exception. These traditional Seattle hippies lived for all of mankind and they celebrated free non-judgmental love. Their followers added orange to the abundance of black and purple.

The New - Age Doceitists (NAD) had their roots

in biblical times and were in close proximity to Silver Trail. Unfortunately they did not share the virtues of the hippies, as they harboured a bad sentiment towards mankind seeing the flesh as inherently evil. They even encouraged their followers to carry out dark physical deeds so that the purity of the spirit could be fully realized. NAD were dangerous and were at the scum - end of this Gathering.

In a fir copse just east of the NAD position were 'Felo de Se' - a suicide cult comprising of members in their thirties. Their followers had black faces - (natural or painted) with dark purple dreadlocks. The name of this sect meant death by one's own hand. This group of people effectively lived to die. This was a tragic indictment concerning the state of society in 2040.

The final group in attendance were another fatalistic batch of young people who were collectively known as Our Beautiful Suicide (O.B.S) Like Felo de Se they had a burning desire to leave life, but they were younger, in their teens or twenties. Many of their members were quite unique in terms of beauty. They had a collective radiance about them and age had not had a chance to wear them down.

The two suicide groups had already seen an upward surge in numbers after the nuclear eradication of Salt Lake City. As the festive season approached, a disproportionate number of people wanted the new year to be their last year.

The Allgood Gathering had massive Online interest. Speculation was growing that with two suicide cults attending, the Jonestown Massacre (1978) cumulative total of deaths (909) may be overtaken. A rather sinister competition was being set up on the net between Felo de Se and O.B.S over who would deliver the highest death-toll. Gallows humour abounded with bets being made and forecasts taken.

The current *form horse* was Felo de Se but OBS had promised to run them close. Security cohorts poured scorn on these death estimates and said that no one would die on their watch. Somehow though, this was already a gathering force that was out of control.

The physical site boundaries of the Allgood Gathering were quite extensive. There were just two days to go until the start of the Gathering and a great range of security checks were being carried out. Some of Kyra's unit had been flown into Allgood as had most of the key players in the MC-Project. The latter had been meticulously researching the life progression of the triplets and the dossier of danger was starting to take shape. Sources stated that Sane planned to address the ranks of the Gathering as he often did. So far there were no indications that the other brothers would also appear.

As night drew in, moonlight flickered over the meadows of Allgood, casting sharp shadows yet blurring form and any firm definition. On the fringes of the site a young fair-haired couple held each other naked on the verdant dew-covered grass. They were both members of OBS, but right now death was the last thing on their minds. The lithe pair were about eighteen or nineteen and they rhythmically sank into each others bodies. She was damp from his touch and her wetness increased when he thrust his strong-veined phallus up her compact vagina. She muffled a sigh as he lifted her higher to engage in a standing copulation. She proceeded to wrap both her legs around him as he stood. She was hungry for his full length and she rocked on his hip region as he grabbed both her arse-cheeks to hold her in place. He easily rocked her slight frame, up and down on his pulsating cock and she extracted a really moist deep-fuck from him as a requited love token. After their mutual climax, his cock started to spit semen over her vulva and then both of them sank to the floor with their sex-sweat glistening in the moonlight. No one had said a word for some time as words can undo the chemistry of a measured fornication and in many ways a good fuck is often a silken silent-movie! The couple stood up once again, embracing each other with an alluring tenderness. Indeed they shared the intimacy of the first-born lovers.

Then a voice sounded - an uninvited intrusion.

"Nice performance folks - any chance of a second demonstration? There were we thinking that you were OBS, but no we must have been mistaken! I mean nobody fucks each other like you two just did if they're on a fucking suicide ticket do they?"

The woman answered.

"Fuck off. This wasn't a showcase for voyeuristic perverts like you guys."

"Strong words Miss Decorum - so which clan are you from?"

The fair haired male lover answered rather indignant at being observed by these uninvited guests.

"OK so we are OBS members, but why the fuck does that matter?"

"It is just the hypocrisy of it all. You have so much life and so much vitality and yet you are going to end it all in two days time. A fucking waste if you ask me."

"We haven't asked you. Anyway which fucking sect are you then?"

When the answer came back, fear ran through the lovers.

"We are NAD guys - any problem with that?"

Before the couple could respond, a hatchet took out the woman and a dagger was impaled through the spleen of the man. As the NADS departed two corpses were left in their wake. OBS already had a

two-nil lead.
Security never heard a word.

SEVEN

On the first day of the Allgood Gathering, the crowd initially looked as if it was going to be smaller than expected. However by midday of that first day, the floodgates started to open and people began to enter the site in their thousands. Whilst the colours of the various sects held a dominance, a lot of non-affiliated groups arrived too, curious to see if the Doomsday predictions of the internet would come to pass. This event had captivated people from across the social spectrum and the collective media placed a very high status on the Gathering. The potential for another Jonestown type of tragedy was high and the OBS cult had received the highest exposure due to the young age of their members.

One good looking OBS member's status profile carried the tagline *Death is my Friend* and this had set the scene for others to follow. Many citizens were at odds with the logic surrounding the suicide groups though. These people had turned up at the Gathering with the express purpose of stopping people killing themselves. They didn't want to see OBS and Felo de Se enlist in the conveyor belt of slaughter that had been forecast. These people stood out wearing white tops and The White-Tops soon became the esoteric name for these would-be lifesavers.

Sharmilla Hendricks and Jasmine Silver were among the first people to enter the site when it opened. They had ditched their formal attire in favour of festival-type clothing for the Gathering, as they knew that it was essential to melt in with the groups for their tracking role. Rumours were emerging that the security forces may arrest Pastor Sane if he made any moves to verbally instigate mass suicide In this climate of suspicion, everyone was watching each other. Sane was due to address the assembly from the Lunar-Trance stage at 10pm that evening and Sharmilla made a point about this start-time to Jasmine.

"If Sane does choose to whip up the crowd under the cover of darkness that could be bad news for us Jas."

Jasmine countered before hearing the fullness of Sharmilla's point.

"Jimmy Jones, David Koresh and most other cult-suicides involved daylight massacres. Why does night give us an extra negative Sharmilla?"

"I feel that Sane has more potency to generate the hysteria that he needs with the claustrophobic aura of the night. He can better weave his sick chemistry from the veiled magnitude of nightfall."

"On the plus side though Sharmilla, it is easier for the faint-hearted to slip away into the night and escape when the bodies start piling up."

"That's true Jas. I love the way that Ms Silver always has a half-full cup! Ever since I have known you Jasmine, you have always stayed upbeat and enthusiastic for our project."

She momentarily lowered her voice as some of the NAD contingent came walking by. After they had passed them, Sharmilla continued.

"Do you ever have down days Jas?"

"Sure - I guess I do. I'm the same as everyone really. In my case - a 53 year-old who has a career that is very fulfilling and doesn't want for much."

"Have you always been Jasmine Silver?"

"No I..." - she stopped, not being able to take her eyes off who was passing by. In a dark suit strode Pastor Sane. His black security cohort flanked him on all sides and they glared at the various groups in the Gathering. The group made for an impressive sight and Sane shone out as a supernatural entity. His forked tongues flickered across his satanic lips and his penetrative eyes made most people avoid direct visual contact. In short, his presence overpowered people and once again he used his mesmerizing appearance to maximum effect. Suddenly he ordered his cohort to stop and he looked directly into the eyes of Sharmilla Hendricks for a good ten seconds. Lust, curiosity and animal instinct exuded from him. Then he clicked his ivory cane for a continuation of the cohort march. His eyes looked back briefly - burning into the very soul of Sharmilla.

When the marchers had moved on and the 'spell' was broken, both Jasmine and Sharmilla were able to fully contemplate the magnitude of what they were up against, The satanic side of Sane had surfaced without much attempt to play it down and both women felt alarmed by their vulnerability in the presence of a central protagonist with coils that were shaping a darkened new America - a darkened new world.

After the relatively close encounter with Sane, Sharmilla messaged Thane Costa-Mendez and Vincent Perry to add to the MC-Project compliment at the Allgood Gathering. Both of them were staying in close proximity to the site and they arrived quickly as a result. Thane's good nature came to the fore immediately.

"I knew that you couldn't last a night without me Sharmilla! Vince and I were betting on how long you two would go without some guys helping you out! Sharmilla assured Thane of the real need for doubling-up on the MC-Project presence and he could tell that Sane had really scared his colleagues. Sharmilla particularly, was made of strong stuff, but the Svengali - pastor had definitely unnerved the joint project leader.

At 19:00 a new security contingent replaced the previous cohort and none other than William Kyra was leading this batch. As the sole Head of security, he still preferred to lead from the front on occasions and he wasn't going to miss Pastor Sane's address for anything. Kyra was one of the most powerful men in the world and he got to pick and chose about what he opted to do. If he encountered any opposition to his plans, he would expunge it like he had done with Kellerman. He felt invincible and yet when compared to Sane and his brothers his power was nothing. That night would not be a reckoning for him, but it would for others.

At 21:30 the security cordon ringed the Lunar-Trance stage area and all the sects were grouped in readiness for Sane's words. The tension was pulsating and a trickle of sweat fell from Jasmine's brow. She felt nervous like her leader did and she trembled slightly as she thought of the double-tongues and his hypnotic stare. She was determined to rise above these fears with a steel resolve. Under her breath she muttered "do your fucking worst - I'm ready for you."

The Lunar-Trance started to reach a new crescendo and some members of the assembly started to sway in rhythmic appreciation. NADS as always, maintained an aloof separation remaining isolated with their unified hatred of everything around them. OBS moved with the dance-culture of youth pulsating through them and even Felo de Se shared a smile before the big push! Judas Silver Trail were very pensive as were The White-Tops who had circulated through the throng. As 22:00 came and went, a fever pitch of excitement for the *main-man* to emerge occured. Even those people that hated Sane wanted his address to begin, so that they had something concrete to project their hatred onto.

The speaker started to slowly emerge from the shadows and most of the crowd went wild in ecstasy. This was their dream-zone - a beautiful fucked-up reality! A chant began that rapped out their adoration. "Sane, Sane - fucking insane!" All over the site the cauldron of sound emanated around, to be hungrily swallowed up by the moving sects. Sane strode toward the Lunar-Stage with his entourage, like a crazy boxer approaching ringside. His eyes pierced through his addicted *flock* and he loved their exultation. Why rush immortality, he thought and he decided to *slice-up* the minutes before duty called and his address began. He adored the foreplay.

At 22:22 the darkest verbal address in American history began.

"I have been talking with God again!"

The crowd went totally manic, punching the air, screaming their appreciation and breaking the hold of *decent* society. It was time for some indecency! Sane continued.

"He tells me that heaven is getting rather sterile - too full of old folks with their restrained moral sentiments. He told me that it was time to rearrange the equilibrium and get more of you youngsters up there!"

A second even more rapturous reception followed, with some of the youngest sect members crying with joy in the process.

"You see guys - you owe this world nothing. It is merely a warm-up stage until heaven is reached. Tonight my beloved, is an opportunity really. An opportunity to embrace the sparkling thrones of heaven early. You chanted for me earlier. Well my friends I have a return phrase for you - my beautiful followers and it runs "Hear the laughter as we leave faster."

A new piece of suicide-vernacular was thus written.

This phrase was repeated time after time as a selection of psychedelic drugs were passed around.

A young recruit in Kyra's security cohort looked quite ashen and he asked a question to his leader.

"When shall we arrest Sane sir? This crowd are buzzing on the bad side."

Kyra's response confirmed what many had thought for years.

"There will be no arrest tonight young man, we'll just let nature take it's course."

Another burst of excitement ran through the crowd as two containers of Devotion-Potion were wheeled onto the main field of the Gathering. These were situated just below the speaker's podium. Sharmilla looked horrified and she said to Jasmine "they're gonna fucking do it - the bastards!"

Jasmine tried to swallow, but her mouth was dry and she was transfixed by the two containers. The said containers had arrived so nonchalantly, as if the contents were an everyday part of festival gatherings and not a suicide-recipe for hundreds of people. Somehow this guise of normality made the suicide preparations even worse. It was almost as if they had been legitimised! Sane started speaking again.

"It is nearly time to let you pioneers go. I will give out the potion with one ladle and my brother Troth will do the same with another. He will be situated over by the fir copse, while I will remain here. We will ensure to keep a tidy site - no Jimmy Jones mess here! Subsequently when you have moved on, your body will be gently carried to the waiting sanctuary tents. There your remains will be treated with the respect you deserve"

A chill ran through Jasmine. The precise finality of everything made her shudder. The OBS followers started to queue up by Sane's location and Felo de Se did likewise in Troth's appointed locale. The nightmare was taking shape and tears welled up in Jasmine's eyes.

Some White-Tops tried to get in the way of the OBS suicide-queue. The most vocal of them yelled out a warning.

"Come on you guys. We've got to stop this fucking madness!"

One of Kyra's men snapped back.

"It's freedom of choice you dumb fucker!"

The White-Top kept on pushing his point, becoming increasingly louder. Then a shot rang out and the White-Top became a red-top!

Jasmine wanted to help persuade some of the OBS members of the futility of suicide, but Kyra beat her away yelling "get back you're too fucking old to join this lot."

At that point an amplified Death-Knell-Drum sounded, ushering those who wished to die to get in line. NADS applauded each person as they moved towards the potion container. They collectively hated humanity and so a death-queue represented a form of victory to them. NADS were at the scum-end of society and were effectively a marker for evil. Just before the first consignment was made ready, Sane briefly returned to his podium to congratulate those who were about to commit suicide.

"Well my brothers and sisters, keep a chair warm for me in heaven. I will be following behind, as soon as the last one of you has left. Unlike Jonestown, we all embrace where we are going. This will be our great journey - adults only with no children to make us think twice. Everyone who drinks the Devotion-Potion has made the choice and like Heaven's Gate before us we are all sound of mind with no forcing whatsoever and no coercion. I love each and everyone of you and now my brethren, it is time to go."

Pastor Sane moved down from the podium and dipped a ladle into the potion. He embraced the first OBS volunteer and then filled his cup with the deadly liquid. Everything was frighteningly quiet. There was no panic and only minimal consternation. The Death-Knell-Drum was then muted slightly and classical music replaced the Lunar-Trance. The OBS volunteer sat down, smiled and then drank some of the cyanide-based potion. After twenty seconds, his breathing started to be exhaled in rasping breaths. He shuddered slightly and started to convulse. He made no sound that indicated any pain. Then he swallowed hard, his eyes rolled white and he breathed no more. He was dead and the first body-bag was called for.

Troth moved into a 3-1 lead after seventeen minutes. His handling of Felo de Se suicides stood on ceremony less than Sane did with his OBS contingent and he used less dialogue in the process. Lanterns and a range of artificial lights guided people between the two suicide-posts. Stacked pyres added further luminescence next to the fir copse location. Occasionally a random shot would pierce the darkness, but usually this just involved a person getting impatient at having to wait in a queue and choosing to end their lives themselves instead. This annoyed Sane and Troth and the corpses of these protocol-breakers were flung with anger into the body-bags. By midnight, Felo de Se had stretched ahead in the body-count statistics. Sane glared at his brother - he *hated* losing.

Sharmilla and Jasmine helped out just beyond the suicide queues. They were able to persuade a few OBS members to turn back, but this had to be undertaken very covertly as Sane and Troth watched events like a couple of hawks. Most people they contacted were not for any suspension of suicide though and were conversely looking forward to it!

By the time the small hours came around, William Kyra had got rather bored with the repetitive applause kept up by the NADS and so he decided to inject a new dimension into events. He activated three Excoriators, carefully making sure that each one was primed for a *targeted* impact. Kyra flung one Excoriator into the arms of a NAD member and the other two were given to a Silver Trail member and a White-Top respectively. None of the receivers had ever seen an Excoriator before and curiosity naturally got the better of them, as Kyra knew it would. They started to fumble with this strange metal device and then bingo - the barbs bore in!

The Nad receiver screamed so loud as his body was *bladed*, that even the drugged-up suicide crews paid attention. The same thing happened with the doomed White-Top, but the Silver Trail member managed to tear his off - at the expense of a couple of fingers! He did survive though, lumbering into the woods like a howling madman.

As the Excoriators gnawed their way through their victims, Sane noticed Sharmilla in the mid-distance and a cold dark smile appeared on his face. She recognized the attraction in his eyes and a fleeting thought briefly registered in her mind. She suppressed it though, as somethings are best kept hidden.

At 03:00 Troth and Sane called a thirty minutes Time-Out so that the piling-up corpses could be moved and placed in body-bags. At this stage, seventy-eight OBS members had committed suicide so far and ninety Felo de Se members had done the same. The White-Tops and all decent-minded people were glad that these figures were lower than predictions had forecast. At this moment, the cumulative total of the Jonestown suicide-toll seemed well out of reach.

Sharmilla was in one of the marquee rest-rooms. She was downcast. Reports had come in that stated Vincent Perry had consumed one of the many free drugs on site. After getting wasted, he had joined up with some Felo de Se friends and had then taken the lethal Devotion-Potion. He had become just another fatality in MC-Project history and his expertise now lay in a body-bag.

The woman reached into her toiletry bag and took out some cocaine. She was very weary and needed a quick Columbian-tonic to recharge her spirit and keep her alert. She formed a pure white line across her hand-held mirror and selected here favourite inhalation-straw from her mobile supply kit. Life was shit all round for her at the moment, but at least the cocaine would bring a form of temporary relief. She then savoured snorting her best white-friend whilst she pondered about who would replace Vincent Perry. The MC-Project were floundering now really. In previous eras the organisation enjoyed a far more hands-on commitment whereby they were more proactive in their own destiny. Now they were just marginalized and were merely a token presence among much bigger players. Since the loss of Europe the MC-Project could only illuminate and monitor criminality and occult presence but the power to prosecute lay solely in security domains, with the project excluded. Sharmilla was so consumed in her thoughts that she didn't initially notice the figure who strode into the rest-room. It was Troth and he came straight to the point.

"My brother may have eyes for you, but my tongues flicker further than his and delve right into the woman. Do you understand me?"

Sharmilla wanted to look away, but she couldn't. She hated what she liked and yet a big part of her knew that this was inevitable. He ushered her into a seat and started to loosen her clothing. She had been watching one devil, but another one had secured her shadow. She was damp for him and she hated herself for her negligence. Who would count the bodies now?

EIGHT

Light crept into the marquee rest-room. Sharmilla stirred and gradually came round. It was 07:09 and she had just started to piece together the last four hours. She remembered Troth's double-tongue referencing and his wandering hands. After that she had no recollection of what had taken place. She was still fully-clothed and no outward blemishes were on her body. She then remembered doing a line of cocaine and the body-count stats of the suicide sects. "*Shit*" she said out loud realising the full extent of mentally drifting on her watch. She raced to the rest-room entrance in a panic and a scene of devastation met her eyes.

The Allgood Gathering was no longer a tidy site. Bodies lay all around in contorted states. The dead lay open-mouthed and all lustre had vanished from their eyes. The corpse of one dead White-Top had been decapitated and five Judas Silver-Trail members had met a similar fate. A few NADS were walking around, but many of their sect also lay dead. Sharmilla moved further into the site and she asked a White-Top what had prompted the large increase in deaths during the last four hours. His answer was very exact.

"Excoriators! When people saw what damage those metal fuckers do, they panicked and a stampede-effect was created. A lot of these corpses were victims of the crush. The Gathering organisers just stood around laughing at the chaos. We live in sick times Miss!"

With that remark he took his leave and Sharmilla went looking for the other MC-Project members.

Thane Costa-Mendez and Jasmine had both been helping victims of the crush. They had both been surprised by Sharmilla's absence to a level, but Thane saw a pattern emerging and he made his views known.

"She goes it alone too much Jas. It will be her undoing one day. I worry about it though, because Sane was showing a big interest in her and that is frightening."

Whilst the MC-Project regrouped, the body-counters set to work. They had orange numbers for the victims of the crush. These victims would be separated from the suicide sects due to the accidental nature of their deaths. Day two of the Allgood Gathering was aptly titled 'picking up the pieces' - a very appropriate piece of vernacular in the context. The body-counters started to filter back reports that suggested the Jonestown cumulative death-toll figure was unlikely to be beaten. This was bad news for the media as they had over-hyped estimates for weeks and now their reporting would just come across as sensationalist blood-lust. Both Sane and Troth's suicide-locations were now 'shut for business' and the queues had now evaporated. The cumulative deaths showed a final result of Felo de Se 312 OBS 288. Jimmy Jones had an infamous record that would stay unbeaten as far as American casualties were concerned. The suicide-push would reconvene in Wisconsin in two weeks time. Thane sent a text of this result and he also asked her location. She in turn had noticed the suicide results and these had furthered her resolve to try and take either Sane or Troth out of the equation. She was still unsure about what had happened with Troth in the missing hours, but that slice of history would stay confined to the corridors of her mind. The right trigger may illicit memory on this occasion, or she could let her project colleagues probe her mind-sight. It was a little ironic that she herself, - the joint head of the MC-Project could be probed!

She shivered a little and dismissed this idea. That, after all was *her* prerogative.

The next couple of weeks were a form of preparation time for all concerned. Sharmilla was set on eradicating the devils and she had a plan to take out one of them. She anticipated that this would be her last act so as to speak, but she felt that she was expendable in such a context. As she drew on a line, she planned the end.

Flambeau in Wisconsin was the venue for the next leg of the suicide-tour. When Sharmilla and Thane addressed the project cohort, all agreed that it was time to go on the attack against the satanic forces of oppression. In her key-line speech Sharmilla didn't mess around.

"I have had enough of watching people wither and fall. We have tracked these fucking devils. We know that at least two of them are scum - the waste product of a depraved society. It is our duty to stop playing mind exploration games and wipe these fuckers out."

Her joint project leader then spoke from the shadows.

"Nice equalisation-sentiments Sharmilla, but how exactly do you propose to do that? I mean, security collect all our guns and blades before each event. What are you going to do - wish them dead!"

"Alright, you can turn off the sarcasm Thane. I have a way to remove one of them. Exactly which one will depend on their movements really, because I cannot forecast which one of them will make advances to me in Wisconsin."

Thane became indignant.

"Advances! - what the fuck are you on about Sharmilla? This sounds like Jane-fucking-Austen to me!"

"No need to get so fucking heated Thane. Wait and see - some things are best kept hidden."

"So you keep on, but I guess that you should open up more woman, 'cos people are dying on our watch."

She did not reveal any more details surrounding her plan though. She would not be drawn any further.

Flambeau was seeing a lot of snow that year and gatherings were moved inside to counteract the adverse effects of the weather. Wisconsin would be a battleground where some could fall on their own sword. That was the one inevitable factor.

Both brothers spotted Sharmilla as soon as she arrived on site. There were several bars and this is where Sharmilla tracked Sane down. She did not make the first verbal move, because she knew that he would...

...sure enough.

"My curiosity never ebbs for you Sharmilla. I wish to go further in our liaison as I am sure you do."

She left things open.

"That's a maybe."

With that he gently took her by the forearm and spun her round to face him. He flicked out one tongue to illicit a response and she made eyes at him with a succumbed gesture. He led her away as she hoped he would. In his chamber, things had been made ready and he led the verbal exchanges again.

"I guess at times an adjunct is worthy of attraction. You are an adjunct Sharmilla - what can you offer?"

Sharmilla made her move.

"Are you as good as your brother?"

With that line, Sane rose to his full height and Sharmilla parted her legs to accept entry. Her vagina was moist, not through attraction, but through necessity. Her plan needed things to be lubricated from the outset. There was no more small-talk and Sane moved the woman, like it was the first time. Then he pounced on her and drove into her vagina with an animalistic ferocity that revealed his true nature. He pummelled into her as though she was taboo - a veritable form of de-marked access. She was his and he would claim her. Then her previous-comparative words excited him still further and he cursed the woman under his stale breath as he tore into her. As he thought of his brother claiming her first he hammered her vulva, she wrapped her legs around him to deepen his entry still further and then his bleeding started. With a final stroke the drips became a profusion and blood splattered across the ornate bed sheets. Then he realised that the would-be hymen was an inserted razor and nausea took hold of him. More and more blood flowed, dripping from the bed linen in a scarlet cascade. He then screamed with rage and dug his satanic claws into the brave MC-Project martyr.

His acidic blood burnt into her belly and she started to die with satisfaction etched on her face. He then withdrew, but it was too late. There had been too much blood loss, too much *red*. In a vain effort, he screamed for his brother and he proceeded to punch Sharmilla's body with fury. She had beaten him and he died knowing it. Unlike his father, alone in Norway, Sane would not outlive his victim in this instance. Sane died spitting his blood across our heroine's face.

Lightning crackled across the sky in a vibrant satanic send-off. Jagged forks tore into woodland and scorched the land with direct hits. As Sane died, scales started to cover his face. He headed for his grave not as a man, but as his true form. Both tongues now fell limp from his putrid mouth. A deathly odour consumed him and then he was no more.

NINE

Troth had heard his brother's scream of rage. As the elements started to change, he knew that Sane was dead. He was incapable of feeling any remorse and viewed the death in cold, matter of fact terms. Now there were just two brothers to continue his father's legacy. Over the last sixteen years Troth had relished scattering his bad seed across America. He loved his first-born status and the extra physical strength that came with it. He may have lacked the mesmerising hypnotic powers of Sane, but he and Scope shared a dominance in securing women. Impregnating women was thus the central factor behind his creation. In this respect, he served his dark master very well.

As a wanderer, Troth wasn't tied to one place for any great length of time. He would arrive, mingle, rape or impregnate. When the latter category was achieved, he would quickly be on his way.

Due to his immense physical strength, he often gained employment in the farming industry. If the weather became inclement he would leave the fields, undertake building jobs and work inside. His good looks ensured that he had a regular supply of women on his travels and that double-tongue was particularly sought after! Usually Troth travelled America as a loner and that often aroused suspicion in the communities that he visited. At times he had to fight his way out of a town with angry residents following him to the state border. His closest call thus far had occurred seven years hence in Oregon. He had quickly risen to the status of Chief farm-hand and had been given a converted hay-barn for his working residence. The local women soon learnt of his locale and his expertise in sexual conquests became the talk of the town. The woman that he fucked most was a twenty-seven year old called Maria. Her white-blond hair and pert lips set her apart from most of the others and some of the locals wondered if she and Troth would wed one day. They had reckoned without Troth though. He wanted to double-fuck both Maria and her younger nineteen year old sister Elisa. When he had first broached this subject to Maria she had refused outright, but over time and during a sustained period of bad weather (light snow in this case), things changed. When he received a text from Maria with an affirmative message, he smiled and threw another log on the open fire in readiness for the arrival of the sisters. There was no building work scheduled for him that day and nothing to do, but fuck really. A light knock on the door signified the arrival of his quarry. The lose robe that he wore did nothing to disguise the huge bulk emanating from his genital area. Both his tongues flickered across his lips as he turned the handle. Troth then ushered both women over the threshold and now they were his!

Maria bristled with sexual confidence as she had been one of Troth's women for some time. Elisa was less assured, being a bit nervous. Anticipation had both of them locked in a state of willing subservience. Whatever he wanted, they would do. Now it was just a case of waiting for his orders of the day.

Troth was also a little apprehensive though. He had a surprise for his visitors that he hadn't tried before. He made sure that the women each had a glass of wine and that both of them had a comfortable seat by the real fire. He announced his intentions to the women, speaking in a softer voice than usual - a beguiling trick that often worked for him.

"Girls you both look *radiant*. Thank you for sharing my fantasy on this *bitterly* cold day. I have been dying to consummate our attraction for each other in a threesome and I have a couple of surprises that I am sure you will like."

With that he dropped his robe to the floor and then smiled at the audible gasps from the sisters when he revealed his double-penis! Troth added a commentary to their view.

"Our sex has always been good Maria, but I chose to retract my second penis thus far. I thought a double-fuck will be a real celebration. You can ride me like a fairground attraction if you like! Symmetry will be our key here. We will release the two embedded full-length wall mirrors initially and you will stand naked in front of them, facing each other. I will sit on the floor between you. When I see your naked svelte frames, each penis will grow beyond your comprehension. Then upon my command, one of you will straddle my left-aligned phallus and the other will do the same thing with my right-aligned penis. Then we will enjoy the rhythm of our locked-in symmetry. Once we are in position, the generated sensuality will take over and our mutual satisfaction will be the outcome. It is now time to lose your clothing girls because I know that you are wet from my words. It is time to breed women of Troth."

The sisters stripped down in an almost choreographed motion and threw their clothing to the far wall. Troth watched them do this and both of his genital organs reached a state of erection. As Troth stood up, each woman grabbed an erect penis and rubbed it across their lips like it was a savoured morsel. As they did this, Troth placed one left hand digit up the vagina of Elisa and one right hand digit up the anus of Maria. Then he asked the sisters to kiss each other and they exchanged tongues with a feverish appetite. They needed no coaxing and their familiarity with each others mouths, showed that this wasn't their first time. If Armageddon was coming, these sisters didn't care!

As Troth finger-fucked his two women into a state of sexual frenzy, each of them came, with their long nails digging into the veins of their chosen penis. Troth was now nearly ready to take his women and he lubed up both his cocks as he prepared for entry. He had fucked over three hundred women in his time and yet each of them was still a savoured experience.

As he entered Elisa he marvelled at the tightness of her vagina and when he entered Maria, her pierced labia sent spasms through his manhood. Then the rocking-copulation began in earnest. With Troth deep in each woman, he pulled them down onto his thighs - the left thigh for Elisa and the right one for Maria. As each woman became more lubricated from his skilful stroke-play, hoarse groans emanated from the pair, with Elisa squealing the most. Each woman then rode her selected phallus into a state of ecstasy. Troth had wanted to cum simultaneously up both women, but he soon sensed that Elisa's tighter vagina would speed things up on her side.

This proved to be the case, although Troth's second phallus shot semen up Maria's vagina not long afterwards. The first ejaculation had prompted screams of utter joy and Maria had echoed her sister's fulfilment, if not quite matching her wild abandon. The three of them sank to the floor in a sleep of contented serenity.

Troth slept with the naked flesh of his women acting as a cocoon of warmth for his *plated* satanic skin. The contented breathing of all three of them continued the synchronicity of their lovemaking. The sleepers drifted for a couple of hours, until a bullet smashed through an upstairs window. Troth was up in seconds and he yelled out some instructions to the women.

"Stay on the floor girls. The shooters will make themselves known. I get some jealous fuckers sometimes. Just you wait and see."

Sure enough, after eight minutes of waiting, a voice through a megaphone issued an ultimatum.

"Some of us are fucking sick of you Mr Double-Tongue. We hate you fucking about with our women. Leave the girls inside and come out and face us - if you dare!"

Troth gazed out of the netted curtains. There were about twenty of them - he made plans to even the odds. He proceeded towards the stairs and in the hall cupboard, he took out a bouquet of mixed shrapnel parts and a mid-distance grenade of Korean origin. He then loaded his Beretta and placed a Semtex-timed charge in the kitchen. These were just precautions - he might not need them. He rolled a makeshift funnel from a Venetian blind and shouted back his reply.

"The girls must leave first. You'll have your parlance with me then. I guess that you guys ain't going to have things any other way - are you?"

His question remained unanswered as he thought it would. The girls had tears in their eyes as they prepared to leave. Elisa asked one question of her new-found lover.

"Is that it Troth. Are those bastards gonna kill you?"

"They'll try and fail as usual, but you two must keep travelling away from here because only my true colours will get me out of this one and you don't want to be around to witness that - trust me! Once I select my second-skin I won't know who I am killing, so you are best kept away. I fired well - I know it - you are both pregnant. I know things that others cannot see. You will never see me again."

With that line Troth opened the door and ushered the women out. The waiting boyfriends drew nearer the barn ready to collect their women, plotting their one-sided revenge as they walked.

Troth laughed to himself. He knew that when a couple of them gained enough courage, they would come and storm the front door. That just charged up his adrenalin still further. His second skin started to kick in and he felt the epidermal changes taking place. He rose upward to his full height, all three metres of it and scales started to replace the flesh on his body. His eyes became over-sized reptilian slivers and his jaws trebled in size. His eye-teeth became protracted fangs and his hands were now claw-based replacements. He had a forked tail that mirrored his forked tongues and although he had never met his father *Klue*, he was a carbon copy of that ultimate beast.

He moved towards the door as eager hands forced an entry. In a demon rage he sprang at the intruders. It was *playtime*.

Claws ripped out the windpipe of the ringleader and the forked-tail spun round simultaneously to decapitate the second in command. The posse then started to open fire, but Troth's plated skin was too tough to be penetrated. A third man was executed via a fang-bite across his face and another died when his spleen was ripped out of his body. Troth directed acidic spittle into the eyes of some other intruders and he broke the skull of his biggest opponent with a head butt that rendered brain-death in an instant. The others ran or crawled away. The women sat transfixed in an intruder vehicle with satanic semen festering in their wombs. They both looked at each other - just wondering.

Troth then left the scene of his massacre and the

house blew apart when the charges went off. The beast kept running, away from his previous lair and sought refuge in the snow covered terrain. This was the place to hide the scents of yesterday. He changed his shape back and sank into the darkness. It was time to leave Oregon.

TEN

The wind swirled around the cemetery in random gusts and Thane Costa-Mendez dropped his bouquet of lilies onto the coffin lid. In a way he felt closer to Sharmilla now, than when she had been alive. She had died a martyr in his eyes and had sacrificed her life by taking out the vile presence that was Sane. How she had done that he would never know, but she would always remain elevated to him now. She had thrown the first domino down and it was up to the others to take out the remaining devils. He scanned his fellow mourners with mixed feelings on his mind. Next to him was Jasmine, who he liked and greatly respected. She had been very close to Sharmilla and was now the last high-level female presence in the MC-Project. A few spaces further back stood Kyra, looking stern-faced as usual and a little portly when compared to when Costa-Mendez had first seen him. Thane loathed him as bad things had seemed to follow the security chief around from day one and he also had a low opinion of the MC-Project. He felt that it was hypocritical that Kyra was at the funeral in that context. He was a bully and Thane hated him.

Paul Santorini was just down the line and he shared some of Thane's views concerning the mourners. Paul had been devastated by the death of Sharmilla, feeling hollow and fearful as a result. She had always made time for the introverted Santorini and his eyes welled up as her coffin passed him by. Although her killer died with her, Paul felt that wasn't the end of things and he wanted to take out the surviving brothers as vengeance on her behalf. The quiet man's anger was beginning to burn and thus even in her death, she made him strong. The remaining project members had all been invited to attend the funeral and most of them did turn up to honor their dead leader. There was a shared feeling among a lot of the project members though that Sharmilla's death signified the end of the MC-Project in effect. They would continue with their current investigations, but somehow the appetite for any new business seemed to have vanished. The project often seemed to bring bad fortune for the protagonists of the organisation and over the years they had paid the ultimate price - death!

As the coffin was lowered into the grave, Jasmine became aware of a pair of eyes scanning her. She recognised the uniform - it was Scope. The glance wasn't either aggressive or friendly. It was more non-committal, as if Scope was curious about something to do with her. Some of Scope's men moved toward his vicinity and he had to look away. He didn't look back, but the link had been made nonetheless. There was an underlying chemistry between them, that neither of them could explain at that moment in time.

The wreaths were then placed on the grave and the mourners funnelled away from the cemetery.

The MC-Project met for one last time a couple of weeks later and the three longest serving project members vowed to keep tracking the two remaining devils. Costa-Mendez and Santorini would pursue the wanderer Troth wherever he went and Jasmine would shadow Scope. The three of them would touch base via text, but each of them knew that they were just tying up loose-ends really and to all intents and purposes The MC-Project was dead and would live only in the annals of yesteryear.

Stalking the wanderer was difficult, as Troth had developed a sixth-sense to detect when he was in a tight corner and he would melt away like a chameleon entity. He could usually head off danger, whether that was radiation in Utah or flooding in Delaware. He always seemed to be a step ahead of a black spot and this was not that surprising as he had been the instigator of several of these danger-zones. The smallpox outbreak in Salt Lake City had been his *masterpiece* so far. Now though, he was the cornered animal. When Costa-Mendez and Santorini tracked him down to some Virginian wasteland, an impasse was created. It was a case of *who would blink first*?

Costa-Mendez was no great shot, but Paul Santorini had seen Navy Seal service and had been trained as a sniper. He was a terrain expert and a superb marksman. He dropped his haversacks down to ground-level and started to build a hide. He used brush, dried wood and foliage. Dead moss clumps were used in addition, to bulk up the structure. Costa-Mendez helped him, but neither of them said a word to each other. After nearly five months of tracking their devil, they had become so accustomed to building surveillance outposts that words were unnecessary during construction. They lay in wait for him during daylight hours. Night was for stalking and both of them knew that darkness presented more *kill* opportunities.

On this occasion Santorini took the first watch, while Thane grabbed his four-hour sleep period. Just over halfway into the period, he awoke - things were not right.

Initially he could not place exactly what was wrong. He scanned his surroundings with his night-vision glasses. Santorini stood five metres away, with his back against a tree. The dim glow of their evening campfire still added a scarlet luminescence to the scene and as his eyes became more accustomed to the dim lighting, he worked out what made the scene unusual. It concerned the absolute stillness of Santorini, with not even a flicker of movement emanating from him. He had gone to sleep on his watch. This was unheard of for Santorini, although Costa-Mendez had been caught out himself a couple of times in the past.

He quietly approached Santorini, being careful not to make too much noise in the undergrowth. As he got closer, he saw that the man, although still standing, was slumped forward. He decided to gently rouse him with a small push to his right shoulder.

The force used was minimal - just enough to make the recently severed head fall to the ground again! Santorini had been decapitated and his head had been put back on his bloodied neck-stump. Troth had been playing with Costa-Mendez, while he slept. He could have easily killed him too, but like a cat playing with a mouse, he chose not to. Cruelty was his foreplay really. A chill ran through Thane, as this devil was opting for a *slow-kill*.

The darkness hemmed him in and pressed his face like a black velvet robe. Since Thane's gruesome discovery, it seemed that the darkness had a blacker pitch - oppressive and uniform in terms of coverage and the eyes of the night seemed as though they were everywhere. Thane's heart pounded and he feared that Troth would detect his anxiety and expose his mortal fears. He sunk to the ground in a primal instinct to hide from his fear. He made himself small and prayed that what he feared wouldn't come his way. He started to crawl through the undergrowth, knowing that somewhere close to him was the severed head of his friend. This angered him and a new found strength was the result. He stood back up, determined not to cower in the darkness any longer.

Then he remembered what Jasmine had given him five months back, to ward off close proximity danger.

He felt that it was a chance in a million, but with death lurking only yards away, he had nothing to lose. Jasmine had come across one online Satanic Protection site that featured the dying groans of a range of animals associated with Satan. Goats, cats, snakes and wolfhounds had been slaughtered to create this site. He activated this acoustic site and muttered *here goes* under his breath. He raised the volume of his phone-speakers to full and then waited.

For a good two or three minutes, no sounds split the darkness and he wondered if Jasmine had been sold a freak-show rip-off. Then the sickening moans of a goat having it's throat slit pierced the night. This was answered with a howl of rage that made Thane fear his end was coming. The slaughter kept reverberating around the clearing and still no attack ensued. After ten minutes, Thane reached inside his backpack and took out a light-flare to add a more powerful source of illumination. He flashed it in the direction of the devil and saw the beast on the undergrowth carpet, with his hands in his ears in a vain attempt to block out the tormenting sound. A chance in a million had just come in. He ensured that the site kept playing the slaughter on a looped continuum and quickly sent a triumphant text...

...Devil down: Hit my Location: Be Prepared - It's Troth.

This was the text that the farming communities of America had been waiting for and they sped to the activated location. As they approached, Thane stood above the devil, with his light flare illuminating the scene, but unfortunately like the downed-devil, he too was becoming overconfident. His signal then momentarily cut out and Troth pounced. Troth rose up and took Thane's head off with one clean serrated blow. Just like Santorini before him Thane ended up one more decapitated victim. Then the phone reactivated and the sound of slaughter returned. Once again the devil fell down and this time he wouldn't even the odds. He lay floored for an hour with the sound torturing him still further. Then thirty guys leaped on Troth beating him with their fists and boots. Occasionally he would manage to kill one of his attackers, but as his enemy built up in hundreds, he knew that the souvenir hunters were just a few minutes away. He managed to metamorphose into beast form during the beatings, but this time it was too late. His strength had largely ebbed away and as many hands grabbed his plated skin, he knew what was coming. He was then bound a hundred times and one eye was gouged out. For a while he was hooded, but they tired of not seeing his beastly jaws and so the hood was then ripped off. Someone then went for some petrol to ignite his funeral pyre, but that was then deemed "too quick" so it too was discarded. In short they were determined to savour his death and drag it out. He had killed hundreds of their number in quick-kill exchanges. They were going to make him suffer - no quick kill from them though as they were going to wallow in death.

And so it was that the second earthly devil was raised up on sticks and paraded through Virginia as a trophy before the pyre was lit. They spat at him and ripped off pieces of his hide. Time after time they would revive him - so he would suffer. They urinated on him and someone even defecated on his plated skin. His one remaining eye looked upwards as some ugly kids and fat mothers leered down upon him. Finally, he was ignited and the flames consumed him.

When his charred remains were exposed after the fire, the locals stamped his bones into the scorched soil and then he was gone.

Troth would have the last laugh though as he had impregnated hundreds of their number and already

the crimson cradles had sprung up throughout
America.

ELEVEN

When the guys were tracking Troth, an unusual bond built up between Jasmine and Scope. She had tracked the devil to Burlington in Vermont and was waiting for him to emerge from a cluster of shops in Church Street Marketplace. A hand tapped her on her left shoulder - he had beaten her to the first move! His voice was deep, but gentle.

"Looking for me, I believe?"

She stepped back, alarmed at the deceptive way in which he had encircled her, without her even noticing. She composed herself, but gave a rather defensive reply.

"Er yes, sorry I didn't know that you were in front of me!"

"How can I help you Jasmine? - If that is your name?"

Her heart raced as she didn't know what to say. She had expected confrontation, not a metaphorical emancipation. His initial decency really flummoxed her and she fell silent. He saw this and re-took the verbal lead.

"This marketplace is my favourite part of Burlington Jasmine. Do you like it?"

"Yes, I guess that I do - it's got character"

"Character?! What state are you from?"

"None. I'm English by birth, but the MC-Project rushed me to the states when my family got murdered decades ago. What about you? What was your route here?"

"Like you Jasmine, through tragedy. My mother died during the birth of me and my two brothers."

She wondered whether to ask Scope the ultimate question. Initially she was too scared, but then she conquered these fears and went for it.

"Do you not know what you are?"

"Sure I know, but you seem so serene - as though you don't expect me to showcase my other side."

"That's right, I don't. I'm just enjoying talking to you."

So that was it. No forked lightening thunderbolts or lugubrious scenery on this occasion - just two people with over 20 years between them, who got on from the outset. The pair of them continued to walk through Burlington, whilst the other MC-Project members pursued Scope's brother.

After the subsequent deaths of Costa-Mendez, Santorini and Scope five moths later, a firm friendship had been formed, with no going back to the old ways in each case. The MC-Project had dissolved and only one devil remained. Scope was still in charge of America's nuclear arsenal, but other forms of warfare had a higher status now and these types were not in his control. America hadn't used nukes in conflict for years and the recent Salt Lake City detonation was seen as a one-off necessity. Only the MC-Project knew of Scope's background and now the last frontline project survivor viewed him as a great friend and not an enemy. Scope was not a threat.

After six months of friendship, Scope decided to ask Jasmine to accompany him on a visit that was very dear to his heart.

"Four or five times a year I journey to Seattle Jasmine, to visit my mother's grave. She was a beautiful woman. There is a life-sized bronze statue of her in the Mount Pleasant cemetery in Seattle."

After a brief pause, he continued speaking.

"Sometimes I see her spirit and yet sometimes I don't. It will mean everything, if you agree to come with me. I'll get the flight-tickets now, if you're fine about that?"

Jasmine felt that she could hardly refuse and so she agreed to meet Scope the next day for her first visit to Seattle. Apart from pleasing Scope, she had another reason for wanting to go to this venue. This pertained to her curiosity surrounding Marcia Levene. She felt sure that Levene was the woman that she had seen with her late father on UK news footage when she was eleven. Scope hadn't made the 'his-mother-her father' connection yet. Things were definitely coming full-circle and Jasmine awaited the next historic-link with interest.

On the plane to Seattle she laughed inwardly, with herself sitting next to the devil in a small charter-plane, just like thousands of others doing internal flights that day. She kept on waiting for some *act of god* to take out this devil and yet the more time that she spent with Scope, the more confident she became. He was decent, kind and sensitive unlike his two brothers and in short Jasmine was loving the time that she spent with him.

A couple of days later, the couple made their way into the peaceful Mount Pleasant cemetery. They passed a cherubic angel initially and then a series of dark grey headstones. There was no bronze at all at this point and then Scope took a right-hand fork into some more affluent parts of the cemetery. They headed straight for the Levene family-plot.

Resplendent as a centrepiece stood a life-sized bronze figure of Marcia Levene. She had always loved her appearance when she was about twenty-seven years of age. Straight away Jasmine made the 'other woman' connection. There was no doubt in Levene's beauty, but Jasmine thought of another woman at this stage - her slaughtered mother Tanya from the massacre that she had witnessed on Herm when she was eleven. Part of her initially saw Marcia Levene as threatening due to the connection that she had established, but then she remembered who her Mount Pleasant escort was and this poor entity had no pictures to build of his mother at all. She felt that his sorrow would buy her silence in this instance. This wasn't easy for her, but the bronze Levene could gaze down as long as she liked - she was dead after all. She recalled Scope's phrase "sometimes I see her spirit" at this stage and a chill ran through her.

The bronze Levene statue stood 177.8 centimetres tall - an exact life-size figure. She was a mistress of all that she surveyed.

Jasmine and Scope then walked around the statue and viewed her from all sides. The most life-like quality pertaining to this bronze statue involved the way that her long hair had been completed. This had been spread tousled across her face as if Levene was celebrating her mane for all to see. The mouth hinted at an open mouthed pout and the superbly contoured cheekbones were another feature that captured the real Marcia perfectly. In hushed tones, Scope paid tribute to his dead mother.

"She's beautiful isn't she?"

"There's no denying that. Bronze adds a lifelike quality to her too."

Jasmine could clearly imagine how a bronze spectral presence could appear lithe in the twilight with flickering shadows interplaying across the statue's face. She wanted to see moonlight bathe the statue and she said as much to Scope. He was pleased with her enthusiasm, but he kept on reiterating that seeing her statue move was an ultimate vision that he had only seen twice. His words were delicate in their coverage of this matter.

"Twilight is starting to drain the light Jasmine, but my cold blood does not expect to see her dance tonight. We will see gossamer-thin spider webs enshrine her statue, but like most nights she will remain earthbound and not sprite like. Only twice Jasmine - only twice."

He looked so mournful that Jasmine took him by the arm and led him to the gates of the cemetery. The pair of them walked away in the now forming darkness and that was a shame, because the spirits did want to play that night, led by a dark-haired Levene, free from her bronze entrapment. She looked for her son, but he had gone now. She flitted between the graves with an almost feline-gait that remembered the yesterdays of a distant place and a distant lover. She was in her element believing that she danced alone - sylph-like for the pleasure of narcissus.

Then the pair returned. She smiled at her son, glanced at the woman and then left the glades of the cemetery. It was time for her to be bronze again. He stayed by her statue all night - the mother he never had. The morning mist then woke our two sleepers. The pieces were falling into place.

TWELVE

The couple decided to lengthen their stay in Seattle and people assumed that they were a smartly dressed mother and son. They took up residence in an upmarket house that was situated in close proximity to Mount Pleasant Cemetery. They never saw Levene's lithe spirit flitting between the graves again, but it wasn't for lack of trying on Scope's part.

As Scope had opted to spend more time in Seattle, he had arranged for a digital mobile support unit to be on hand so that he could monitor the nuclear arsenal that he was responsible for back in Vermont. He had a team of fifty people who looked after the storage of the missiles and when Jasmine showed an interest in this area, he made her au-fait with missile types, distance, potency and radioactivity. When he communicated with his crew back in Vermont, he would place his left hand on a computerised register screen to begin or end his access. That read his DNA via his skin status and his pore density. After a few weeks he initiated Jasmine into his support team as an invited member. Her left hand, iris-match and speech pattern were all inbuilt into the register screen database and as she toured the digital Nuke Site online, she discovered that Scope had created prioritised access for her in all areas barring the C.O.T.O subsection. One morning she asked about the nature of this excluded area.

"What does C.O.T.O stand for Scope?"

Coils Of The Overkill. It basically highlights the potential options concerning an all-out nuclear war."

"What do you mean *potential*?"

"Each missile has been given a potential status that measures a *target-strike* likelihood. So if for example a missile had a Moscow (4) status, it only has an outside chance of detonating in Moscow. Other factors would probably thwart the progress of this missile. If a missile conversely has a Moscow (1) status, an outright successful nuclear strike is very likely. Every missile has a journey to undertake that is digitally assured from it's inset and the more grade (1) projections we get the more likely we are to win an *Overkill* situation. In our worst envisaged situation, an Overkill would involve significant Nuclear arsenal usage where many missiles are used by all sides. In effect that would almost certainly signify our end - a total wipe-out."

Jasmine found C.O.T.O fascinating and so she reeled off another key question.

"So in that context what could trigger C.O.T.O and make the missiles start to fly."

"Some country going past the agitation stage and firing first. Everyone has always assumed that Russia will start things off , but China, North Korea and a range of other rogue countries could well be the catalyst - even we could!"

"We are hardly *whiter than white* are we ?"

Scope then took Jasmine on an extended virtual tour of some of the missiles and he explained 'blocking options' as a method to thwart incoming missiles. He even indicated at this stage that America could fire from the space of another country, triggering conflicts in distant regions making a country believe that it had been fired upon by another country. This he called a 'bluff-strike' and he said that it had taken place twice under his watch. In short he said America gets what America wants and he wasn't holding anything back from Jasmine.

He kept returning to a Peking (5) site and

eventually explained why.

"This site looks as though it is hardly front-line in terms of it's danger to the States - I mean it carries a (5) status right now. The thing is though, the Chinese keep altering it's status by bringing in the Heavy-Nukes. As a result last month they were up to a (2) and we had to shift some of our long range Nukes in Idaho to match them. They are playing cat and mouse with us really, but at least it keeps us sharp in the process. Moving the big Nukes around always carries a potential for problems and the Chinese know it. They are like a little man prodding Goliath!"

Jasmine continued with another question.

"Who has clearance to launch a missile?"

"As the Head of the Military I could in my own right, but otherwise it will be determined by The President, a Security chief like Kyra and a Humanitarian - overseer. The latter is thus a form of three-way approval. During the Salt Lake nuking a while back, I let Kyra take lead for once, but I feel that the President is starting to see through William now, so I would be pivotal if something similar were to happen again."

The couple developed a greater understanding of each other's nuclear motivations in the ensuing weeks and both of them really enjoyed working things through together. After quite a short learning process Scope decided that it was time to raise the profile of Jasmine in military circles.

"You'll be pleased to know that I have cleared you in nearly all nuclear-sensitive areas now I put your name forward for a position of a Humanitarian Overseer and this was uncontested. So there you go Jasmine - welcome aboard."

So it was decided that Jasmine undertook a new role at the behest of the *third devil*. He was the antithesis of his two brothers though displaying humility, decency and a soulful passion for doing the right thing. As time advanced, Jasmine felt a real bond with him and this magnified with each sharing experiences together. She enjoyed travelling around Seattle with Scope on the Open Tram Network and they would regularly use this method of transport to get about. The day before they were due to return to Vermont, the couple decided to enjoy one last ride on the trams. It was Jasmine's way of saying thank-you for her new found role.

As they neared the Tram terminus, a group of children ran ahead of them, laughing in a carefree fashion. Unfortunately though for some youngsters, the trams had become part of a Dare-culture, whereby a child would stand on the open tram-rails for the longest possible period, before jumping away to safety in the last possible seconds. This infuriated the drivers who swore at the kids who took such liberties with life. On this particular day one ten year old girl was earning her *dare-colours*. Her mum was away and she had sneaked out to join the others. She watched an older boy jump clear with two seconds to spare. This was close, but she vowed to do better. Some policemen then moved the group along, but they all reconvened at a different section of track. This was where Jasmine and Scope were heading. The cold afternoon added a veiled-yellow light to the scene and the pair smiled at each other when the tram-stop was reached. Whilst waiting for a tram, they initially talked to each other about their impending journey back to Vermont. Jasmine had hired a sturdy Four-by-Four vehicle for their route and they were both looking forward to a 3000 mile long journey. Suddenly Jasmine's eyes widened in horror when she saw a young girl standing among the rails The tram was approaching fast, but the warning scream that she wanted to give, just died silent in her throat. Then

Scope seized the initiative and with just seconds before the potential collision, he sprinted ahead and with both palms, *pushed* the child to the other side of the rail and safety. In the momentum he fell headlong and his outstretched hands both landed across the rails. They were severed in an instant and then the screaming from the onlookers started.

The tram had made such a *clean-cut* that the bleeding didn't start for a few seconds. Then as the screams reached Scope's ears and the tram shuddered to a halt a bit further away, things gathered pace. Jasmine collected the severed hands and the blood then started to be released, spraying out across the tramway like a couple of red fountains. Some of the aforementioned juveniles tried to staunch the blood of the man who had saved their friend, but unfortunately some others started laughing. Jasmine saw this and screamed out at the offenders.

"You fucking cunts - this guy just saved *your* friend's life!"

The offenders slunk away and Jasmine tried in vain to put a pressure point on each bleeding wrist stump. Scope whispered to her amid the chaos.

"Jas - now you listen my friend. I will change back soon - I can feel it. Take my left hand, discard the right. The kids can have a fucking souvenir! You know the C.O.T.O stages and I hope you never need them, but you know what to do."

He cut his words short and some of the children displayed alarm as his plated skin started to emerge. His metamorphosis was beginning and as some scales started to replace his flesh elements, a crowd started to build up with a omnipresent mob rule mentality. His lifesaving act had been witnessed by many people though and fortunately most of them saw him as a hero and opposed any execution in this instance. As Scope started to metamorphose further, this floored devil tried to stand, but the crowd told him to keep lying flat, because his blood loss increased each time he raised his profile. His speech was now very rasping and as the medics arrived, he spoke to Jasmine for the last time.

"Jas - it's nearly time for me to return back. I've loved the time that I have spent with you."

Jasmine cut in - addressing the medics.

"Come on guys. You can save this hero. Come on do your fucking job!"

In her panic, Jasmine's tears raced down her cheeks. She bathed the brow of the dying Scope as the pulsing blood proved impossible to contain. As death approached the tell-tale second tongue emerged for a last time. His dying words were profound and were addressed to all who were assembled around him.

"Well guys - *showtime* is nearly over! Go beyond first impressions will you? A devil on the outside isn't always one on the inside. Keep this sacred. Well Jas I love you. I guess that now it is time to meet my revered mother."

With that line his lids closed and many of the assembled hung their heads in a mark of respect. In this case death had been the ultimate leveller and Scope's demise was uplifting in that context. Scope's remains were taken away by the medics for the most part and his body was eventually placed beside his mother's grave in the Levene family plot. Now they were together.

For her part, Jasmine vowed to honour him in her heart for always. After his funeral she decided to drive the route back to Vermont that she and Scope would have taken. Their drive had been planned and she would follow that through. She headed for the open highway with resolve in her heart and a severed left-hand in the car's ice bucket!

THIRTEEN

President Hudson paced The Oval Office like a madman. He felt that his beloved America was falling apart around him and he planned to tell Americans what he thought in a *State of the Union* address that he would call. He intended to pull his people back into the moral fold and he simultaneously wanted to warn them of darkened forces that seemed intent on stealing them away. He would evoke halcyon eras when his country had stood firm against tyranny and threats. He linked this to a *state of play* analysis concerning where his country stood now. Over the next couple of days he modified the address several times. When he eventually finished it, those people who were chosen to hear a test reading thought that it was succinct, poignant and accurate.

He chose to present his address on the front lawn of The White House so that this ultimate American symbol was right behind him when he spoke. His words would be televised to a global audience and thus although his focus was for the American people, other nations would receive his opinions. On the day of his address, he approached the speaker's podium in a nervous yet determined state of mind. He began his address.

"Fellow Americans. These words don't come easily for a President in his first term of Office. What I will say hurts me to my core, but it is a true sentiment of how parts of American society are falling away into the mire. Due to our free-hand liberalism, we have allowed a culture to develop where some of our young people queue up in respectful lines to commit suicide. Their motivation at a recent gathering in Allgood Alabama was to fast-forward their way to heaven.

They were cheered on to their deaths by Satanists and other sects of vile beliefs. I ask you good Americans - how did this type of evil pollute our society? Who let these perverts in to our society and who turned a blind eye?"

He momentarily paused and looked straight into the camera, before continuing.

"What scares me the most is the way that these sadists and suicide squads have been allowed to exist without opposition alongside respectable Americans. Obviously when Jonny joined a suicide sect his neighbours didn't want to bother Jonny's parents. They preferred to observe the First Amendment and let things ride out. Now I *shout* at you moral Americans that I do want to bother Jonny's parents and shake up the *whole* neighbourhood. I want to be a President that notices and I want to get involved. If I get in your face then I am doing it for a moral reason and I am tired of looking away. Both Houses have affirmed my decision to make these suicide sects illegal and I won't rest until they have been eradicated. So it is time to stop peering through those net curtains and stand up and be counted. We need to regain a clearer moral America and everyone must be key in this transitional process. We have been stained by evil presences and some of that contamination is located in places that are usually beyond suspicion."

He paused again to sip his water and paced slightly to his right, before continuing.

"Another area that seems to have been undone by sadistic impulses, involves some of our security forces. It seems that certain black-clad units have become a law onto themselves, administering unprovoked beatings to innocent people. Worse than that has reached my ears, involving one security chief who takes great pride in hurling torture devices at people for kicks. These weapons are like barbed metallic-lobsters and they embed themselves deeper and deeper into a victim. Once mechanically activated, these devices start devouring the victim that they land on. I will ensure that this *sick* sport will cease forever from this moment forward and the person responsible for using them will be severely dealt with. It is a sickening state of affairs where people that you rely on for help, abuse you. Depraved security chiefs have no place to exist on anyone's watch - including mine."

He then chose to reiterate the key points in his address and then he added to them.

"So first the suicide-tours and then the security lapses and finally the most dangerous S-word - Satanism! Many of you decent Americans will recently have come across individuals who profess to be devils or satanic offspring. I am not going to glorify them by naming them, but in my Father's day, devils came and went and died like the rest of us - hardly elevated in that context. We were led to believe that these entities possessed a power that was far above mere mortals, but I keep asking where are they now and I laugh at the answer."

Watching from close by, Jasmine scowled at the President. She agreed with him with regard to the first two satanic brothers, but definitely not the third brother. She had loved Scope. Indeed, he was the reason that she was there, having been asked to attend by none other than Hudson himself due to the humanitarian role that Scope had chosen for her. *Little did the President know* thought Jasmine and she laughed inwardly at the way that Scope had broken satanic stereotypes in the short time that she had known him. In her opinion, he was *better than them* - including the President. Hudson continued with his address.

"Just over a year ago, I had to give the green light

to contain the smallpox outbreak in Salt Lake City via the use of a nuclear missile. Many thousands are now believed to have died as a result of this explosion My heart hangs heavy for the victims, but there was no other choice. New information pertaining to this contamination has now come to light. It seems as though this outbreak may have been manufactured or deliberately created."

He paused for maximum effect before resuming in a more subdued tone.

"Some of our stockpiles of germ warfare are missing, including a consignment of smallpox phials and it is highly likely that someone deliberately used one of these phials in Salt Lake City. We are redoubling our efforts to relocate the missing stockpile and we will scour our land until the consignment is found. You see my fellow Americans, what irks me most about this tragedy is that the contamination came from within, with some *vile* source willingly contaminating our own landscape. We can't even blame an external terrorist element because no cell has claimed ownership of this atrocity. This leaves a bad taste in the mouth with Americans killing Americans being the most likely conclusion that we can draw. It is time to seek inspiration from the history books my people. Back in the 1960's the phrase *Love America or Leave America* was created and the same vernacular is appropriate now. So, if you want to usher Americans to their deaths - leave! If you want to brutalise Americans in the name of security - leave! Finally, if you have hidden satanic agendas - leave!"

The crowd outside The White House applauded at these words and it was some minutes before the President was able to return to the podium.

When he did, he directed his attention to Jasmine.

"Not all my news concerns dark negatives though.

The Memory-Camera Project has closed down after the sacrificial deaths of two of it's protagonists and whilst this seems like another negative factor their deaths must be measured by the associated deaths of the satanic forces that they were instrumental in killing. They showed that this type of societal scum are not invincible and the project thus died as an example of a great sacrificial American institution. A final gesture to the said organisation has been made though, with the promotion of Ms Jasmine Silver as a humanitarian adviser for the late Commander Scope's unit. His brilliance will be remembered in her appointment and subsequently as one candle is snuffed out another re-ignites."

More applause took place after this announcement and although The MC-Project had now officially been laid to rest, a new American heroine had emerged from the ashes. In his closure President Hudson had an emotive appeal for his people.

"So my friends, if you are approached by satanic pariahs, *stand bold* and face them off. If the high and mighty embrace obscenity, pull them back to restore serenity. We are back at a new cross-roads America. It is time to re-invent morality.

"God bless you and may God bless America."

To some people Hudson's speech was an upbeat call for a new moral awakening, but for others it was a collection of typecast metaphors. In effect, America was still split.

One positive outcome of Hudson's speech concerned the immediate arrest of William Kyra. He was briefly incarcerated, but then found enough funds to post bail. He had a list of serious charges awaiting him, inclusive of murder. His beloved Excoriators were also impounded with him being under suspicion. On the day when the consignment of torture-weapons were driven away, Kyra watched and smiled to himself. *Fuck them* he thought, as he still had one Excoriator hidden away. Kyra was then placed under house-arrest and lawyers haggled over his future, knowing that his trial would be a lengthy gold-mine.

The former security chief started to become very rotund with only the occasional visit of his son breaking this monotony. He started to drink far too many Jack Daniel's bottles and crashed around the house in a very dishevelled state. Pretty soon the one time neat and organised Kyra became almost unrecognisable. His possessions lay scattered across his house in an uncoordinated mess. After three months of house-arrest he engaged in a particularly heavy bout of drinking. After his third giant-sized bottle of Jack Daniels had gone down the hatch, he tripped over a rug edge and landed face-first among some of his possessions. He tried to right himself, but fell again and this time the familiar metallic love-call of an Excoriator reached his ears. Due to his drunken state, he couldn't initially place exactly where it was, but then it locked-on and proceeded to skewer him through his left flank. He screamed out in agony but no one heard his anguish. The Excoriator ignored his heart and proceeded to slowly munch it's way upwards towards his neck. Kyra released blood, spittle and vomit as the Excoriator paused briefly before sinking it's metallic hind-legs deep into his neck. It then sucked the power of speech from him and it menacingly slowed down as it gouged out his left eye from it's socket. With no power of speech and only half his eyesight, Kyra prayed mentally for the end and as he did so, his efforts to escape the device became more and more frantic. He fell into broken jars of vinegar and when contact was made with his wounds, he went into a temporary pain-driven seizure. The Excoriator shifted it's position to the back of his neck and the metallic clippers were set in motion. He tried to rip the Excoriator from his neck, but lost four fingers in the process. Then the fat man's heart finally gave out and he became blue-faced within twenty seconds. The Excoriator continued ploughing up the dead man - a truly *fitting* end for a man who worshipped sadism.

He had one mourner at his cremation.

FOURTEEN

Jasmine fitted into the missile-surveillance unit with ease. Scope had shown her the rudiments of her role back in Seattle and her additional humanitarian duties involved her researching demographic factors in target areas. Scope's left-hand identification logging point and his desk area had been left in place as a mark of respect for the late Commander. His favoured grey trench-coat sill hung from the back of his black leather chair and his digital workplace area still carried gold embossed lettering with his name on it. Jasmine regularly brought in some flowers in memory of her dead friend these added an element of beauty to an otherwise monochrome environment. She got on very well with her unit colleagues, although she started to feel rather isolated when compared to the rest, with her role being to minimise casualties while the others seemed to adhere to a seek and destroy prerogative. On occasions she would surf the missile status-sites like she had done with Scope and she felt more at home observing the bluff and counter. Bluff tactics surrounding missile-movements that she did with humanitarian aid. Her colleagues noted her affinity with this area and eventually it was decided that she should undertake the same role as the others. She was pleased to leave her old role behind her and she started to excel in the metaphorical chess-game surrounding an Overkill situation. Her work station was next to Scope's *shrine* and one day she inquired about how long his work-space would remain unchanged. The reply from a senior colleague surprised and yet excited her.

"Oh Scope's work-space will stay just the same

indefinitely - a mark of respect for sure, but also it must be stated that his unit cant be closed down because the activation key to force closure is missing.

Jasmine played dumb, although she knew the answer to the question that she asked.

"What kind of key are we looking for?"

"Scope's left hand. He lost both his hands in the fatal accident that befell him and the left one activates his work-space and could shut down Overkill - or activate it. Many would argue that Scope had the only real trigger-potential because he could act alone by using it. Now we would need a three-way agreement just to move missiles let alone fire one. Gone are the single-strike days. We have gone too soft."

The man's name was David Jackson and Jasmine thought that he spoke with a slightly wistful air with regard to past days. She wondered if Scope had ever gone beyond the chess-piece stages and actually fired a missile - she hoped so. His reply surprised her.

"Sure he did. I know of four occasions when Scope went past the bluffing-stage! Two Russian subs were taken out - one in the arctic and one showing too much interest in our west-coast ports. He also nuked part of Brasilia to put a halt on Brazilian superpower growth and he sent a massive nuke to Baghdad as target practice! The latter really wound-up the Russians! You see for the most part we flex and they *run*. The beautiful thing about Scope was that he would often do the unexpected and our enemies couldn't work a behavioural pattern for him - even we know that! Scope was a loose-cannon in many ways, but boy, we all miss him."

That conversation proved to be the start of a firm friendship between David Jackson and Jasmine. He was a couple of years older than she was and had the aforementioned senior status in terms of surveillance. Jasmine learnt a lot from him and occasionally she would glean more historic information about the late Scope's style of rule. She hadn't told a soul about what macabre secret was wrapped up in her freezer at home, but nonetheless she was keen to determine if a *dead* hand could still activate Scope's frozen work-space. She asked Jackson several 'what-if' type questions about Scope and after waiting for the right time, she went for the big one.

"One thing has always made me rather curious about Scope's left hand identification sensor. If it was found now David, would it still work and open his work-space?"

Jackson smiled at this bizarre question, but gave a full answer nonetheless.

"It's probably rotted away by now wherever it is. Even if we found it tomorrow I am not certain that it would encode correctly in the work-space area or not. You see I don't know whether the hand was responsive via a living wrist pulse or skin pore DNA. If it was the latter it could possibly work or reactivate. Interesting witchcraft!"

David Jackson had enabled Jasmine to delve more thoroughly into Scope's world and although he wanted more than Jasmine did, their bond strengthened over the ensuing weeks. As his birthday drew nearer, Jasmine had an idea that would please David, but more importantly provide a clandestine method to sneak Scope's dead hand on site. She was determined to see if Scope's work-space would reactivate. She kept her plan secret and nobody knew about her ulterior motive surrounding birthday-steak celebrations. She still needed to build up a mental picture of Scope's work-space to channel her expectations before she sat in the 'cockpit.' She chose to ask another colleague further Scope-related questions as Jackson may become suspicious of an over repetitive line of inquiry. She subsequently directed her question to a younger surveillance worker called Austin Clements.

"So Austin, what different features did Scope's work-space possess then?"

"Obviously the Direct-Engagement button was a key difference - lucky bastard! Then there was the Exit-Locking facility that he always activated when he fired for real. There was a left-hand dial to enable Work-Space-Destruction (WSD) in cases of extreme emergency and finally an attached Pod that would carry an exit statement should our base be destroyed. The latter has a orbit-penetration strength, so I guess that it is able to withstand everything including the aforementioned WSD. This Pod will stay intact even if there are no people left to tell the tale!"

Jasmine laughed at Austin's gallows-humour. She had got what she wanted from him.

As the birthday drew nearer Jasmine bought five massive steaks in readiness for the occasion. She was glad that America always prided themselves on the size of their steaks - it was easier to conceal objects within them when need be! She thawed the dead hand out on her kitchen table and re-applied an eighth coating of preserving formalin. She was determined to make sure that no trace of decomposition could emerge and spoil her best laid plans. Hiding the hand within the giant steak was extremely intricate as she had to part the steak like a second skin and cover all human traces. Concealing the finger-nails proved to be the most difficult part of this process, but when she was finished one even fatter steak was the result. She was confident that security wouldn't detect her stuffed steak when it was surrounded by other steaks of sizeable proportions.

Jasmine would have a window of opportunity to get to Scope's work-space without being detected if things went to plan. She would cook the steaks in the large work kitchen on the day and then she would present them to Jackson and three other colleagues. It was her surprise for his big day and it made her wider intentions very covert. After consuming their food the guys would briefly depart to another annexed building to take part in more birthday celebrations. Jasmine had been invited to join the others in celebration, but said beforehand that she couldn't go at that time because she would need to survey a particular missile site in that time slot. The others understood as each of them had a specific case load of sites to keep a eye of scrutiny on. It was the nature of their job. This would be the said window of opportunity for Jasmine.

When the actual day dawned, Jasmine's pulse seemed to have a double beat due to the enhanced adrenalin coursing through her body. As she journeyed to the missile-surveillance workplace, she wondered what her punishment would be if she were caught. After a few seconds of reflection she concluded that it would almost certainly be the death penalty - due to the magnitude of what she was carrying around and the ultimate power contained within this object. Her journey had parallels with another woman unfamiliar to her from a distant time in a far off place. She too was a *seer* in that context. She neared the corner of no-return and her heart fluttered like the last caged dove.

Through the doors she went and Security smiled at her heavy load. They glanced inside her haversack and with inane smiles asked if there was any chance of a free steak. She passed them by on the road to deliverance, but now she needed to maintain her envisaged synchronicity.

"Yo - the steak lady!" Yelled Austin, already half-cut in celebration. He laughed, gave Jasmine a buddy-hug and then he sought out the birthday-boy who was proving elusive. The drunken state of her colleagues helped Jasmine and they pushed their steaks around their plates in a lazy fashion, with their desire for more alcohol proving to be more exciting. She kissed a drunken Jackson on both cheeks and hurried all of them away to their next booze-soddened destination. They were playing into her hands really and now it could be Scope-time for Jasmine. She approached his work-space with less caution than before because she had managed to lose the others. She proceeded to tear the hand from the polythene safe-bag and wiped the encrusted formalin from it's surface. She wiped the hand on a towel that she had brought with her and then held it close to her heart with some memories of pleasant times. She drew his chair back and feasted her eyes on his vacant work-space. It was her *now or never* moment and she hurriedly made sure that the Primary activation points were in place and she then placed the dead hand on the activation pad. If Jackson was right about the wrist-pulse, it would be a *no-show* and initially that looked like being the case. The sounds of merriment a few buildings away disrupted Jasmine's thoughts and she scowled at The Master's silent unit. Then a flicker became a screen and the screen revealed those beautiful options. It was time to attack and his spirit would ride with her.

She activated immediately and chose *Direct Engagement* without a second thought! She was gunning from the outset and was loving the experience. She launched an *actual* missile at a projected Moscow (2) site and smiled at her initial efforts. Then she made sure that all exits were sealed and diverted another missile in the direction of north-Korea. Nothing would stop her now. Some alarms sounded from outside, but Scope's palace could not be scaled. She enabled a nuclear sub to engage in a repeat - strike program with Peking. She off-loaded 2 massive 4-Meg missiles from subs off the Japanese coastline. This was proving fun for Jasmine and she smiled again at the metaphorical board-game in front of her. After an hour or so, she concentrated her efforts on blasting Russia from all angles. Her philosophy now was very much *bang-bang bye-bye* and she became oblivious to any moral closure. Then after nearly three hours of engagement came the *warnings* that she had expected...

Idaho Alert State (1) - Attack Imminent with incoming missile in a state of Lock-on. This was followed by New York - Attack Imminent - three incoming Missiles Locked-on. She started to rock in her chair and began to chuckle to herself. She had a speech to prepare to set the record straight and as news of Cincinnati being blown to pieces reached the web, she began drafting her chosen words. As missiles hit her screen from many directions she hit the C.O.T.O button and committed America into emptying it's nuclear arsenal. That signified the end and she knew it. Sirens, alarms and the sound of gunfire provided a dying soundtrack. Red alert warnings ripped into a sonic death - knell. It was time to die.

EPILGUE

Many years ago my little family were cruelly wiped out by the Memory-Camera Project. They left me as a token survivor while the blood of my Father, mother and little brother ran as one across the sand. I swore to avenge the murder of my family as I watched them breath their last on Herm. I am sorry this took so long Daddy, but some things are best served cold. I feel that I, Rachel Vain (not that awful Jasmine that they gave me) have carried out the ultimate vendetta really haven't I? By the time you get this Pod I will be scorched out of existence. You see my friends the Project died in the end but it left me unfulfilled and so my revenge switched to killing you America. You spawned the MC-Project and I have killed you in return.

Goodbye world Goodbye America.

THE END

By Steve Hammond Kaye

About the author

Find *Steve Hammond Kaye* on facebook:
www.facebook.com/stevehammondkaye

I started writing book one *Thirty Four Minutes Dead* in 1990 and concluded the said novel in 1998. I deliberately chose to write the book in a style that is intricate, expansive and visually aware. I wanted the book to engage with the reader in a similar fashion to film on occasions and thus my plot arteries were often determined by a heightened visual perspective.

On the 25th April 2001 *TFMD* was available online for the first time with a publishing company based in Milton Keynes, UK.

Two years later, book two, *The Scream of Feyer* found its way online. This book really is *TFMD*'s *ugly sister* and is a completely different beast. In fact, if it were a animal and you fed it, it would literally bite your hand off!

I wrote this at a time when my life was pretty wild to say the least, so I suppose a strange duality transpired with *The Scream of Feyer* being the mutated offspring.

Book three, *Coils of The Overkill* comes 12 years later after the success of books one and two on Amazon. I'd always planned it, but really knuckled down in 2014 to finally finish The Memory-Camera Project once and for all!

With Kind Regards

THE FOLLOWING LIST OF PEOPLE HAVE BEEN
REMEMBERED WITH HIGH REGARD BY THE AUTHOR FOR A
VARIETY OF DIFFERENT REASONS. SOME ARE VERY WELL
KNOWN TO ME WHILST OTHERS TOUCHED MY HEART IN A
MORE FLEETING INSTANCE. EITHER WAY, YOU ARE LOCKED
IN MY HEART AND I THANK YOU.

MRS AMANDA KAYE: EMILY DANIELLE KAYE:
GEMMA LAUREN KAYE: SALLIE-ROSE KAYE:

PROFESSOR MICHAEL MARSHALL KAYE:
ANNE MARGARET KAYE: ANDREA KAYE:

STEVE MULLINS – MY MATE AND HEAD OF
ICELANDIC OPERATIONS: (STEVE-MULLINS.CO.UK)

HANNAH CUNDALL:

CARLA LANZON:

EMILY ALICE WILSON:

ALEX ADAMS:

JASON BEAMAN (MR COVENTRY):

ROB SHAW:

RUSSELL MORELAND:

DAVID GREENMAN (KING OF THE EXTRA MILE):

ICE CREAM BEN:

MARK COUPER PHOTOGRAPHY:

PAUL ANDREWS:

JAYNE - QUEEN OF THE VETS:

STEVE CAPELL:

ANTHONY MINGHELLA R:I:P

TONIA CANN:

KEVIN JENNINGS - I THOUGHT OF YOU AT THE
END OF COILS BUDDY!:

JUSTIN MASON:

ROBIN ALLEN:

LEWIS WILSON:

MICK HAILES:

ANDY WILLIAMS:

CAREY NELSON:

ANTHONY SIBLEY:

HILTON HARVEY:

GEORGE & ~~JENNI~~ WILBERT:

GARETH WALKER:

LIAM MOODY (MAN OF HONOUR):

MATTHEW MOSS:

DAVE JUPE:

STANLEY BOWLES:

GABRIELLA HAMMOND:

SERA LEFROY-OWEN:

KATE VALENTINE:

JACKIE SWINSON:

KRISTEN SCOTT-THOMAS:

MS C CAMPBELL:

COLETTE FRENCH:

MR T:

TONY FICETO:

PETER CAWLEY (SUPERB ENGLISH TEACHER):

BECCA CHEETHAM:

C.JENKINS:

LORRAINE BEVAN:

LOUISE HARRIS:

GEOFF SAUNDERS R;I;P

MARY SILK:

MARY MOORE:

LINDA SNAITH:

VICTOR PLUMBLEY R:I:P - A TOP BLOKE VIC MATE
GOD BLESS:

STEVE HAMMOND KAYE

Published by

STANDARD CUT MEDIA

Publishing for the twenty-first century author.

Publish your book today - publishing@standardcut.co.uk